Controlling Stakes

JULIA FISHER

Julia Fisher

Copyright © 2025 Julia Fisher

For the straight A students, the model employees, the ones who have it all together.

Be a good girl and turn your brain off for a little while.

Trigger Warnings

Controlling Stakes is a high-spice BDSM romance, which includes:

- Explicit language

- Explicit on-page consensual sexual content

- Explicit consensual BDSM scenes and impact play

- Consensual power exchange/dominance and submission

Chapter 1
Liam

"Don't even think about it," I warned Ben, my CFO, as he reached for his phone. Well, CFO, co-founder, brother-in-law and, once, my best friend. We were still close, but he'd been usurped.

His eyebrows hiked almost all the way to the top of his shiny, shaved head. "Yeah, tell me again why our unofficial COO is missing the biggest meeting of the year?" He was still reaching for his iPhone on my desk as if calling Ava would get her here in time for our meeting in ten minutes.

I smacked my hand on top of his cell before he could pick it up. "Because she has a doctor's appointment, and her health is more important than some meeting."

He leveled a flat glare at me. "Personally, I would have picked a different day to let her play hooky. I'm surprised she even left the building. It's not like her to let you handle something like this alone."

"She's not playing hooky. She's receiving medical care. And as I told Ava yesterday, we started this company ten years ago without her help. I'm the CEO. I don't need a..." The buzz of a phone sounded on the polished mahogany of my desk. Not his, mine. "...babysitter."

A sigh gusted out of my mouth as I put the call on speakerphone. "Yes, Ms. Anderson?"

"The user numbers are incorrect." Ava's voice sounded strained above the New York City street noise in the background. "I just got the email from the research team."

"For VestedAI?" I clicked my computer to life.

"Yes, for Vested. Why else would I be calling you panicked? You haven't gone into the meeting yet, have you? This will affect the evaluation." Her voice was high, breaths coming in little bursts as she wove her way down some city sidewalk.

"Ava, take a breath. The meeting hasn't started yet. How much of a change are we talking?"

Ben launched forward, scrambling to write down the numbers Ava started throwing out like she was a supercomputer.

I grinned at the phone. Sometimes, I thought she kind of *was* a supercomputer. "Okay, we'll look into that. Thank you."

"I'll forward you the email from research. Don't forget to ask about the—"

"Ava," I warned. "You are supposed to be taking the morning off."

She went silent, and I sat forward in my chair. *Don't do it. Don't you dare—*

"You know, this is a routine thing. I'll just cancel, get a cab, and be back in the office in, like, twenty."

"This appointment has been on your calendar for months, and just last week you told me it took you weeks to get on the doctor's schedule."

"Yeah, but maybe I can find an appointment later, on a day when the biggest deal in Wildes's company history isn't on the line." She huffed, and I could picture her so clearly, striding down the sidewalk in her spiked heels, throwing silky, black hair over her shoulder. Her pouty lips would be pushed out in a frown, high cheekbones touched with the slightest flush of anger. Irritated and gorgeous.

Whoa. I yanked my brain away from the thought. I had strict lines when it came to Ava Anderson, and I never crossed them. Not even in the privacy of my own mind.

"It's just an introductory meeting. I've done hundreds of these. I don't need you to hold my hand through everything." Questionable, but I didn't necessarily want to voice that out loud. Not while she was already spinning out.

"Liam. We are in the middle of selling three businesses, and about to launch the next fundraise. Everyone wants VestedAI. If we get this...it'll change everything. I should be there."

"You should be where you are. You are too important to this company, to me, to neglect yourself. You did that once, remember? I won't let you do it again." I nearly growled into the phone.

"But this is diff—"

"Ava." As soon as her name barked out of my mouth, I wished I could take it back. It was out of place, out of character, even. A voice I hardly used anymore, and *definitely* not at work.

Ben's head snapped up from his hasty notes, eyebrows shooting up again to his nonexistent hairline. I dug my fingers into my eyes as silence crackled over the line.

I cleared my throat, coughing out the rest of the domineering tone that scorched my esophagus, an apology on the tip of my tongue.

"You're right," Ava spoke before I could, sounding a little surprised and breathless. Shit. I hadn't meant to speak like that to her, but she'd been taking on too much. These days, she collected new projects faster than I could offload her work to other people.

I was having a hard time keeping up with her, and it sent alarm bells ringing in my head. She'd been getting stressed recently, and she didn't need her boss yelling at her.

"I didn't mean to—"

"No, I appreciate it. You're right. I'll be in right after."

"Ava." I took care to say her name softly this time. Quiet. Like a normal person would, but she had already hung up. I tossed my phone back onto the desk while Ben finished punching the new calculations into his iPad.

"I'm starting to think we need to give her another raise," he commented. If the guilt and worry weren't eating me up, I'd have smiled. He was a good man, a good friend, for not grilling me about my uncharacteristic snap at Ava, even though the room still felt awkward and stilted. Damn. I needed to get a handle on that. Maybe it had been too long since I'd let that side of myself out.

Perhaps a visit to the club was in order.

I pushed the thought aside to consider later. I didn't let that life mingle with this one. "Probably. But if we give her too much, she'll get suspicious."

Ben squinted, mouth quirking in a smirk. "Does anyone get suspicious when they get more money?"

"Ava does. And will. But...still. See if we can find a way to make it happen. Maybe more options."

Ben's smirk turned into an out-and-out grin. "You know how much easier my life would be if she just let you promote her?"

I swiveled my chair back and forth, staring out my glass office doors to where her desk sat empty. "That hasn't worked the last few times we've tried." I was losing count of the promotions she'd turned down.

Ben tented his fingers in front of his face. "Just saying, I might have to get creative. Starts to look bad when your personal assistant makes more than the managers."

"She's more than my assistant, and everyone knows it."

"Everyone but her," Ben clicked his tongue. "I dream of the day she lets us officially make her chief operating officer, and we can stop tip-toeing around this."

I rubbed my forehead. It would make my life easier, too. "This is what she wants, Ben. She might be doing COO work, but if she wants to call herself an assistant, she can. She can call herself the grand fucking czar of intergalactic space for all I care. Ava Andersons don't just fall from the sky. I'll do what it takes to keep her around."

"She's going to find out eventually," Ben warned, his dark brown eyes looking worried. "When we make these upcoming sales, she's going to see how much bigger her equity is."

"Yeah, well," I drawled, as if this exact issue didn't keep me up at night. Ava could run from her past as hard and fast as she wanted, but eventually it was going to catch up to her. I just hoped to hell we didn't get bitten, too. "We'll cross that bridge when we come to it."

Ben rolled his eyes, murmuring something I didn't quite catch just as my intercom beeped.

"Sir? Mr. Masters is in the main conference room for your ten o'clock."

"Thank you, Cheryl." I stretched as I got up from my chair, enjoying the easy flex of my button-down.

Ben tended to sport a suit-and-tie, but I'd vowed when we'd created Wildes Capital that I wouldn't operate like the snobby, stuck-up Wall Street yuppies I'd grown up with. The same ones who turned me down for internships and business opportunities just because of my tattoos, or the fact that I didn't take shit from other people.

Vapid, shallow, and short-sighted. The finance industry was changing, and I was leading the charge. Ben and I had started Wildes ten years ago with some seed money, a few business degrees between the two of us, and a dream. We were still small, but we were growing at a pace almost no one had expected. And this deal with Mark Masters was going to be one more feather in our cap.

Winston, Ava's Rottweiler mastiff mix, jumped to his feet when I stood, tongue lolling. "Let's go bag a new client, huh, boy?" He stretched, claws flexing on his custom orthopedic bed before he trotted over to slobber on my chinos.

Just after Ava was hired, I'd overheard her hissing frantically into her phone about her dog walker ghosting her. It had seemed like an easy offer to tell her to bring the dog here for a few days while she found someone new.

I'd expected a terrier or something, not one hundred and forty pounds of lean muscle and Winston's stunning underbite. But I'd gotten a very up-close-and-personal look when he'd rocketed out of the elevators on his first day and tackled me straight to the ground to lick every inch of my face.

Ava had been horrified, and Ben had laughed so hard he'd nearly peed himself.

A week later, when she found a new dog walker, the office had unanimously outvoted her, and Winston had been a fixture ever since. The staff liked having him as a mascot, and he liked the pets and treats he got when he walked around.

Besides, he made Ava happy, and I tried not to think too much about the lengths I would go to if it kept her that way.

Winston padded beside me as I walked, glancing into the conference room in the middle of the maze of cubicles on our main floor. The glass walls allowed me to take stock of Mark Masters and his entourage as I approached.

His black hair was slicked back, and he was lounging, foot propped on the table, lazily pushing his chair left and right.

"Mark." I swung the door to the conference room open, Winston trotting in ahead of me. "Glad to see you. You know our CFO, Ben. And this is our office dog, Winston."

Mark pushed back from the table as Winston invaded his personal space, sniffing him up and down before moving on to the man and woman sitting on either side of him. "That's...quite the office dog."

I shrugged. "What can I say? He's a rescue."

"Personally, I was hoping your pretty assistant would be here taking notes instead. But I can settle for a mutt." He patted Winston's back, snatching his hand back when the dog turned to sniff him again. Masters's beakish nose wrinkled. "Friendly."

He was too busy avoiding Winston's jaws to see the displeasure shoot across my face. Ben raised an eyebrow at me before leaning over to shake hands with the other people in the room.

I fixed my frown, giving Masters one more shot to correct himself. "Ms. Anderson *is* very valuable in meetings like these, but she had another appointment. She may join us later."

Mark snorted, eyeing Winston as he settled on his *other* custom orthopedic bed. He had no less than five around the office. Ben wrote them off on our taxes. "I don't doubt it. Everyone knows how *close* you keep her."

I lost the war with my facial muscles and scowled. I knew Ava's unorthodox position was discussed up and down Wall Street, but most people only had to meet her once to understand why I kept her around. And Masters had met Ava multiple times.

"I work *closely* with Ava because she's a Stanford MBA graduate who could run your company and mine with her eyes closed."

Mark raised his hands in surrender as the woman on his left looked down at the table. "Sorry, bro. Everyone assumes you two are—"

"Not even once. Bro." Every word shot out of my mouth like a bullet, cold and biting in the glass conference room.

"Ms. Anderson is a valued member of our team. We don't allow that type of misogyny around here." Ben's voice was firm, but he managed to sound more reasonable than I did.

Still, Mark paled, unease flickering across his face as he gulped and glanced at Winston. "Sorry...I mean..." His hands dropped into his lap. "You know how other PE guys are. Just locker-room talk most of the time. I assumed that was the vibe here."

"You assumed incorrectly."

Mark inched a finger under his collar. "Obviously. I'm sorry, of course. And I'll apologize directly to Ms. Anderson." He pulled at his tie until it sagged across his neck. "I've done my homework, and you're the ones I want to partner with. I'm just...nervous. And I apologize. When Ava gets here, I'll—"

"No need." I leaned back in my chair, studying him. You didn't get as far as I had in business without knowing how to get a good read on people. My extracurricular activities further sharpened my senses, allowing me to better analyze people's wants and needs and reactions.

Mark's body language was tense and insecure, and, if I thought about it, had been since I'd walked in here. Maybe his earlier posturing with his leg on the table had been just that. Posturing for his business partners. Maybe Winston hadn't been the one to set him on edge.

"For the sake of our conversation today, just know that what you've heard is true. We do things differently at Wildes. Don't expect the norm."

"Right. Of course, Mr. Wildes." Mark nodded so vigorously, he nearly dislodged his slicked locks.

"Liam is fine. Now, let's get started."

"First and foremost, some updated numbers on your users..." Ben tapped around on his tablet, and I let him take the first few questions.

VestedAI seemed to be the perfect fit for our portfolio. Their algorithm provided sound investment guidance and automatically built financial plans for a low cost. Solutions like Vested were poised to upset almost every inch of the finance industry, and I wanted it so badly I could nearly taste it.

Me and every other PE firm in the city. Vested's valuation had been climbing all year, and it had Unicorn Status written all over it. If we could bag them, I had no doubt the return on our investment would be game-changing. I was going to make a lot of people a lot of money.

As long as Mark Masters behaved himself from here on out.

He relaxed the more we talked, and had ready responses and updated figures that answered nearly all of our questions. I told myself to relax, too. To stop replaying Mark's earlier comments in my head.

Because I couldn't afford to ruminate on how beautiful and charming and perfect Ava was. And my business couldn't either.

Chapter 2
Ava

"Motherfuuuuu..." The elevator whooshed up to the eleventh floor, and I had mere seconds until the doors opened. Mere seconds for me to suck up the pain and stand like my insides weren't trying to climb out of my belly button.

I heaved a breath into my lungs, holding the oxygen in as I straightened, just in time for the doors to open. Three expectant faces stared back.

Cheryl shouldered her way past the other two, thrusting a coffee at me with one hand while Post-its fluttered on every finger of the other. "Morning, Ms. Anderson. We've had a few calls."

I let the breath leak out of my mouth, forcing myself to walk behind her. Walking was...fine. Moving around was...fine. I assured myself of this, forcing my body upright as much as possible while Cheryl rattled off names and client updates. Wesley from marketing and Trina from research trailed quietly behind.

"...and Cameron Hawks called again for you. Twice."

"Great, thank you, Cheryl. This wasn't necessary, but I appreciate it." I waved the coffee at her.

I'd nearly died when Liam had hired her as a "secondary assistant." Wasn't I doing enough for him?

"I'm not replacing you, Ava. I'm shoring you up. We're growing too quickly for you to take everything on by yourself." He'd insisted, but I

couldn't help but see Cheryl as my own personal failure. I hadn't done enough or *been* enough. Liam thought I needed backup.

Even more demoralizing: I really, really liked Cheryl, and if I were a C-level executive, she'd be the exact person I'd want for the job. Experienced, competent, and poised. She didn't spew opinions like a piñata all over the office, like I tended to do. She stayed after five if we needed her, but she mostly came in on time, left on time, kept everything organized, reminded me of things before they slipped through the cracks, and could have been doing much more than I had currently assigned her.

"Ava, you said you wanted the files for the Holmes presentation as soon as you were in the office." Trina finally saw her opening and took it, thrusting a folder into my face. We usually worked in digital, but Holmes was old-school, and I catered to my clients' preferences.

Cheryl intercepted the files. "Did the team update the chart on page eight?" Trina froze, eyes going squinty, before thumbing through the pages. She threw her head back and groaned at the ceiling. I wanted to do the same. I'd forgotten about the updates we'd made last night to the graphs.

My heart sank, and I reminded myself that my job was not in competition with Cheryl's. *Even though I should have caught that.* My abdomen gave a twinge.

"I'll have a new version printed ASAP. Hang tight!" Trina was already sprinting back through my office door, Doc Martens clomping past the cubicles.

"The caterers for the founders' dinner just canceled on us." Wesley's eyes darted between us and I grimaced, partially at the ungodly pain still ricocheting around my stomach and partly because *crap*.

"The one in three weeks?" Cheryl's eyes narrowed as she gently took my work bag from my shoulder and started unpacking it.

"I can..." A sharp eyebrow rose, and she glanced at the coffee, then back to me. I took a sip like a good girl.

"Yes." Wesley wrung his hands.

"Hmm. You should try the team we used for the startup mingle a few months ago. They had good canapés. Or I can compile a list of some reputable companies for you to peruse. Help you come to Ms. Anderson with a solution, instead of a problem?"

That eyebrow somehow got sharper, and Wesley cowered. "Sorry, right. We can do that. I apologize, Ava."

"Wes, we're managing this event together. It's alright that you come to me with issues like this." Did my voice sound strained? Was the room spinning? I set a hand down on my desk. I didn't have time to pass out today. "But..." I glanced at where Cheryl was setting up my laptop and organizing my files even though she totally didn't have to and I *didn't have time* to fixate on whether she was just being nice or if this was a power move. "Do look into that place from the mingle."

"You got it, boss!"

"I'm not the...ugh." He was already gone. "Cheryl, I can do that."

"Enjoy your coffee and just sit for a moment, Ava. There are a couple of emails that came through I want to flag for you."

I bit the inside of my cheek, standing awkwardly and trying not to double over while Cheryl clicked around on my computer. I focused on my office instead. Two large sliding doors off the main floor opened onto the generous space. My desk stood front and center, flanked by two sunny windows. On my left were the doors to Liam's office.

Anyone who wanted to get to him had to go through me, and I kind of liked it that way. It made me feel...protective. Which was probably how an assistant should feel, right?

He was sitting forward at his desk, talking on the phone. His dark hair was swept back from his face, the tattoos at his wrists and neck barely peeking out from behind his button-down shirt. He was something to behold. Full lips, light brown eyes, sharp jaw, a straight, knifelike nose... and all of it was focused squarely on me.

The surge of prickly, giddy heat that worked its way up my belly, that was a super normal boss/subordinate feeling too, yes?

Gah. Don't think about the word subordinate, *Ava.* I waved my fingers weakly in his direction.

"All set. Ava..." Cheryl trailed off. "I don't want to be rude, but you don't look so good. Maybe I could—"

"I'm fine!" I blurted, too loudly and too quickly, because if this woman tried to assist me any more, I would die. "I'm fine. I just need to talk with Liam. Thanks, Cheryl!"

I grabbed my laptop and the files she'd meticulously fanned across my desk, probably obliterating a perfectly efficient organization system, and ducked through the glass doors into Liam's office before I could hear her response. Liam held up a finger as he listened to his call, but I was hardly paying attention, seeing as my baby had leapt up from his bed to greet me.

"Hi, buddy!" I whispered, setting my armload down on the conference table. Liam had more space than me, obviously, and the long room boasted the table, a couch and chairs, and a minibar. All of it was sleek, modern lines and pale wood, except for his ridiculous antique desk, which dominated the far end of the room.

I leaned down to scratch Winston's ears and was nearly brought down by the wave of pain that surged through me. "Ah!"

I hunched over as my abdomen cramped like a motherfucker.

"Ava?"

Winston licked my face, making everything a lot stinkier and slobberier than it needed to be in this moment of weakness, and then he was abruptly hauled out of the way. Liam's arm closed around my waist.

"Sorry, I..." My words tapered off in a truly pitiful whimper, and suddenly I was airborne.

"What the hell?"

"I'm okay," I gasped, trying to focus on the fact that I was in Liam's arms as he strode across the room, and not the fact that my uterus was staging a full revolt, and my ovaries had just joined in. I breathed deeply as he sat me on the couch like I was precious and breakable. He crouched in front of me, hands painting soothing circles across my thighs.

"You're white as a sheet and in obvious pain. I'm calling an ambulance." He shoved Winston out of the way. My pup just sidestepped him and jumped to settle onto the cushion next to me.

A laugh bubbled out of my throat, ending in a groan. The wave of pain was subsiding, but it still wasn't fun. I grabbed his forearm before he could pull out his phone. "It's alright, I swear. All normal."

His brows furrowed, fierce over warm amber eyes that saw too much. "This is not normal. What was that doctor's appointment for?"

"Don't worry about it. I want to hear about the Masters meeting before Holmes gets here." That would be nice. Get back on level footing of work, professionalism, not his thumbs circling the tops of my knees.

"Ava." A shiver nearly shot through me. His voice was close, so close, to that growling, commanding tone he'd used earlier today. The one that had made me sit up and pay attention and...*obey*. "I'm not talking about work until you tell me what's wrong."

"Can I, uh, have some water instead?" He leveled me with a look that told me he saw through my puny attempt at redirection.

"Are you going to tell me what's going on?"

Dammit. "Fine!" I rolled my eyes, leaning closer, challenging. If he wanted to get into my personal life, I'd get into his personal space. "I got a new IUD put in, and it hurts like a bitch, alright?"

His face didn't change, but he looked at me for a long moment. Long enough for me to realize just how close we were. Mere inches separated our noses, and if he turned his head and I tilted mine...we would practically be...

He cursed under his breath, pushing up from where he knelt on the floor. I flopped back onto the couch.

"Yeah, careful what you wish for, Captain Intrusive. Happy now? Now that you know all about my lady parts?" I crooned, making Winston's tail wag while I played with his ears. He lifted his giant head to lay it in my lap. I braced for pain, but it never hit. See? Better already.

Liam glared over his shoulder, yanking a drawer on his minibar open before striding back to hand me a bottle of water and three tablets of ibuprofen. "I don't care about your lady parts, Ava. I care about you being in pain. They didn't give you anything at the office?"

"The patriarchy, dude. They said I could take something over the counter before my appointment, but they don't give you anything at the procedure."

"And you, of course, superhuman marvel that you are, decided you can't feel pain and took nothing."

I toasted him with my water, downing all three of the tablets in one gulp.

"Ava." He sounded softer this time. Less grumpy and demanding. More like *what am I going to do with you?* I had some ideas, but mostly I just hoped he didn't think less of me for taking off work for a girl procedure and then not handling it well. "I'll call Holmes and cancel."

Like that.

"Absolutely not. It's some cramps, and we don't live in Victorian times, I don't need to convalesce. I can take a few meetings."

"Holmes is just the beginning. We've got a full slate, because we always have a full slate, and if you need to rest, you should."

A rising simmer of anxiety tasted acrid in my mouth. First, the VestedAI numbers were off, and I'd missed the Masters meeting altogether, then Cheryl was dealing with issues I should be handling...canceling a meeting with our biggest investor? Not an option.

"Ava." He'd stilled in front of his desk, peering at me with those perceptive eyes. "Do I need to send you home?"

I gulped a bubble of air and let it sit in my lungs. He was offering, for real, to order me out of the building, and it was on the tip of my tongue to take him up on it. Because maybe, just maybe, his command would override my own hectic thoughts, and I'd be able to actually relax for the first time in weeks. His eyes narrowed when I took a beat too long to answer.

"No. The painkillers will kick in soon, and I'll be fine. Seriously, Liam. Trust me on this." It was hard to maintain eye contact, but I did my best, willing every inch of my face into placid calm. His opinion meant everything to me—too much—but that was yet another problem I didn't have time to deal with today.

"If you're sure..."

"Anderson! Liam catch you up on the Masters meeting this morning?" Ben shoved Liam's office doors open, a harried Cheryl close on his heels.

"Mr. Wildes, I told you to wait so I could see if the other Mr. Wildes was ready for you," she chided, clipping primly across the room to hand me...oh.

I accepted the hot water bottle, warm to the touch, and the bottle of Advil she presented, along with the coffee I'd abandoned on my desk.

"Cheryl, *thank you*." I whispered, a little mortified but so grateful I could cry, if I were any less stubborn.

"Remembered that appointment today was at the OB. Put two and two together. Let me know if you need me to reheat that, alright?" The woman winked as she straightened, brow raising in Ben's direction again. "Next time, you wait. Yes?"

"Yes, ma'am." Ben had the good sense to look sheepish as Cheryl strode across the room and pulled the doors closed behind her. "You good?" He nodded at the hot water bottle I maneuvered over my stomach while Winston grumbled and settled with his butt backed up to my hip.

"Yeah," I sighed, the heat already working its way through my body. Between this and the painkillers, my day was looking up faster than anticipated. "Don't worry about it."

"Lady parts," Liam chimed in, settling on the other side of the couch to rub Winston's ears. Ben stuck his tongue out in a gag.

"Men are pussies," I informed him. "And no, I haven't heard anything about the Masters meeting because Liam was being high-handed and controlling. Give me the high points."

"He's a dick," Liam scoffed, scratching under my dog's chin. My heart sank.

"What?" The biggest deal of the year, and Masters had been rude to my colleagues? We had too much riding on this for anything to be less than perfect.

"Well, I think we got off to a rocky start. He was nervous," Ben added.

"He *said* he was nervous," Liam clarified. He and Ben shared a look that made me think they'd already debriefed on this without me.

"You think he lied about being nervous? Why?" I glanced between the two of them, searching for a clue. "That doesn't make sense.

Let me meet with him separately, see if I can get a read on him one-on-one."

"Not necessary. Any time we meet with him, I want the full team there," Liam cracked his neck, like it felt tight. I needed to book him a massage soon. With several big sales and a new fundraising round on the horizon, everyone was stressed.

We finally had a strong track record of lucrative deals, but we'd need something big to make our investors put up more money to help us expand. Taking on VestedAI would be the coup of the decade. We'd land one of the hottest deals of the year, right as we raked in millions for our clients.

It was a perfect storm that would set us up for more investments, more market attention, and more success.

We just had to make it until then.

"If you're sure…"

"I am." He definitely sounded sure, so I didn't push it.

"Mr. Wildes? Mr. Holmes is here to see you."

"Thanks, Cheryl. Can you do me a favor and clear Ms. Anderson and my schedules as much as you can today? Anything internal, let's move it later in the week."

Cheryl, old enough to be Liam's mother, looked at him like he'd helped an entire busload of older adults cross the street. "Of course, sir. I'll be happy to."

"Liam," I began to protest, but he rose from the couch, already waving at Reginald Holmes as he walked into the office. I shut my mouth, knowing better than to berate my boss in front of a client.

"Reggie, my favorite investor. Hope you don't mind, we're taking meetings from the couch today. Ava's had a minor injury and needs to stay low."

My cheeks flamed as Reginald swung his head to me, white eyebrows bouncing above his spectacles. The last remaining heir to a truly massive pharmaceutical dynasty, he came from a long line of rich white dudes whose sole purpose was to make the next wave of rich white dudes richer. In principal, I should have hated him, but he was a different breed. His legacy included shifting his family company's focus to providing foreign aid and expanding access to cheap generics in the states. He was still loaded as hell, but he spread the love.

He worked with Wildes mostly to invest money to fund the medical scholarships he'd created.

"My future CEO has been injured? Wildes, how could you let this happen?" Holmes pulled my hand between two of his. "You say the word, dear, and I'll whisk you away. You want a corner office? Burly men to carry you around on a palanquin?"

I laughed, squeezing Reggie's hand before pulling away to pat the hot water bottle. "As tempting as that sounds, it's just a...pulled muscle. Nothing a bit of heat and rest won't cure."

"Undoubtedly, but it probably wouldn't hurt to double your salary and have a private helicopter at your beck and call."

"Reg, we've talked about this. My personal assistant isn't up for grabs." Liam motioned for the other man to sit. "We know how valuable she is here. There's no way we're letting her go."

I wanted to smile, to sink into Liam's words, but if he knew the truth, that I was barely hanging on, always just on the edge of dropping one of the twenty-seven-thousand balls I was juggling, he wouldn't sound so sure.

Chapter 3
Ava

Friday night, and all I wanted to do was rot on the couch, but a little Marilyn Monroe lookalike was giving me grief about it.

"I'm serious. Let loose a little! You're approved; your most recent test results are cleared. Go have some *fun*, Ava!" Whitney, my across the hall neighbor, pouted as blonde curls swayed across her shoulders.

"Not tonight. I'm exhausted," I whined from her sofa, watching her get ready for her shift at Dragon and running one of her silk scarves through my fingers. The whole place was decadent, tapestries and rugs, soft lighting and the sultry, earthy scent of patchouli, laced with something feminine and alluring.

After spending my days with wannabe alpha males at my last finance job, moving across from Whitney had been a gift from the universe. She was girly and soft, and she *got me* in ways few other people did. My lust compass didn't swing in the female direction, but if it had, I'd have locked Whitney down in a heartbeat. Instead, I'd opted to make her my best friend, not that she'd needed much convincing.

She ruthlessly used mine or Liam's names to get into some of the most exclusive bars in New York, studying her craft, and the competition. On the nights she wasn't spying on other bartenders, we took walks together or curled up for a Gilmore Girls marathon.

When Whitney offered me a night on the town, it was usually an automatic yes, but not tonight. Not...there.

"Please don't tell me this is about Liam. You know I can't speak about club patrons, but I have told you before, he hasn't been in for months." She turned back to her vanity to sweep more blush across her cheeks.

Suddenly, the prospect of heading over to Dragon and letting off some steam was more appealing. New York boasted its fair share of sex clubs, but the only ones worth knowing in the BDSM world were Eden and Dragon. Both owned by Mistress Giselle, who was easily the most beautiful and intimidating person I'd ever met, each location catered to a specific clientele.

Eden operated more like a nightclub, a place for like-minded people to meet, mingle, and maybe take someone home later that night. It was a fun, easy vibe that made dipping your toes into the lifestyle seem more accessible. Plus, the dues were lower.

I'd been a member at Eden for nearly three years and had the time of my damn life there. Being with people like me, people who didn't see my needs and fantasies as taboo, but as a normal expression of healthy sexual curiosity, was intoxicating.

When Mistress Giselle had called months ago to let me know a former Dom of mine had recommended me to be considered for membership at Dragon, I'd nearly fallen out of my chair.

Because both clubs might have been owned by the same person, but that was pretty much where the similarities ended.

Dragon's membership fees were exorbitantly expensive, and the club hosted a wider, more specialized array of events. Private rooms, more intense exhibitions. And who could forget Dragon's most famous feature: its concierge matching service. Mistress Giselle prided herself on finding her clients the best partners, or groups of partners, to scratch their particular itch.

Even though I could afford the dues thanks to my generous salary and company-wide profit-sharing, I still hadn't said yes to the invitation that had been issued months ago. As Dragon's best and favorite bartender, Whitney couldn't understand why I kept my pending approval to the sex club, well, *pending*.

"It's not about Liam. Alright, it's not *only* about Liam," I hedged when she glared at me in the mirror. Because this was only partially about Liam and my deep fear that I'd run into him there. And the mixed feelings I had about what might happen after that.

"Ava, you're a player, and you've been personally invited to the city's most coveted playground. So, go play."

When she said it like that, it seemed like a no-brainer, but I still wasn't sure. "Work is too hectic right now. If I go to Dragon, Mistress will want to match me with someone, and new relationships take work. And *time*." Time I really didn't have because we were frantically trying to sell off companies, maintain all the others in our portfolio, and land the white frickin' whale of the year, too. "I don't want to commit to more than I have to give."

Whitney sighed, capping her mascara and giving Winston well-deserved pets and affection as he passed by. "If you just want one night, why not go to Eden? It's been *months* since you've had any fun, and you know what they say about all work and no play." She rose with the grace of a Greek goddess to slip on her heels.

"I don't have time to play." Winston collapsed on my stomach, and I grinned, rubbing his ears even as the breath whooshed out of my lungs. Who needed air when you could get cuddles?

"That's. The. Problem." Whitney speared a finger at me, gliding across the room to perch on the couch. "You're running yourself ragged. I don't care if it's Dragon, or Eden, or taking up with a freaking run club. You told me what happened the last time you got too caught up in your job. I don't want you to go through that again."

A nagging, poking feeling entered my brain, right in that part of the prefrontal cortex that said, *"I told you so."* Whitney was right. I was burning out fast, and I'd been feeling it for weeks. For God's sake, the only time I'd taken off in the last year was to swap out my IUD a few days ago. But there was just too much pressure, too many projects, for me to take my foot off the gas.

Sooner or later, it was going to be a problem.

Some people can face hard times at work and tough it out, power through and come out the other side like a shiny, unbreakable diamond. Other people...

Well, other people have a panic attack during a client presentation, and end up in the hospital.

"I don't want that to happen either." Sometimes, right before I drifted off to sleep, I could still feel the cold scrape of an oxygen mask being shoved over my mouth. I made a face. "And I'd rather die than join a run club. But I don't want to go back to Eden."

Whitney petted my shoulder. "Good. You're too pretty for cardio, and too good for the loser club."

"It's not a loser club; it's just more...introductory." And there was nothing wrong with that. After all, it had worked for me for nearly two years. There was something powerful and breathless about existing in a place where everyone was learning and experiencing new, exhilarating things.

But Eden was Dragon's more accessible counterpart for a reason. After two years, the faces changed, but the experiences didn't. People joined the club, learned a lot, and then either settled into what they knew, or ended up at different clubs with more experienced members who could teach more, give more.

And I'd washed out somewhere in the middle. I knew my limits, and what I liked, and what I wanted to try and to experience, but I still had a lot to learn. I was too well-trained for most of the Eden crowd, with zero interest in taking on training a fresh, new Dom. Maybe it was selfish, but submission—giving over my control—was what really drove my love of the scene. I couldn't free my mind if I was making sure the new guy tied the knots right.

But I also didn't know if I was ready for something like Dragon. It demanded a level of dedication I wasn't sure I was willing to give.

"I know Dragon can seem intimidating, but we're very open to new members. And yes, new D/s relationships *are* work, but people find partners just for the night all the time over there. Mistress could have you in someone's lap in no time flat. You'll have fun."

That did sound...lovely. "Of course I will; it's like BDSM Mecca. But that still doesn't solve the other problem."

Whitney's eyes grew wide. "Oh, you mean your superhot, mega-rich boss you're in love with? You're right! What if he sees you there, being all hot and submissive and the woman of his dreams? What shall we do?!"

"Winston, bite her." My mutt didn't even stir from where he sprawled on top of me. I rolled my eyes. "I'm serious, Whit. He doesn't know I'm in the community, and he never will. It would be catastrophic."

Whitney scoffed. "Liam Wildes is an established Dom. You don't get the kind of reputation he has without learning about discretion. It's not like he can judge you. He'll be there too, you know."

"It's not about him judging me. It would change things between us, and things are good right now." Things were perfect right now.

After I'd hyperventilated myself right into the hospital, my old firm hadn't known what to do with me. Half of them snickered as I walked through the halls, and the other half treated me like I was a bomb about to detonate if someone spoke too loudly.

When I'd quit on my therapist's recommendation, I'd taken a few months to really think about what I wanted. And I kept coming back to private equity. I liked the business of it, the game, the strategy. And of course, the money wasn't bad either. My therapist hadn't been wild about me diving back into the PE grind, but I'd gotten creative. Maybe a different role at a firm? Not partner track, but still close to the action?

Liam's job opening for an assistant had been more than I could have hoped for. I'd told myself he wouldn't even consider my application, but I'd gotten a call for an interview that same day. When he'd raised the point that I was too qualified for an assistant job, I'd assured him my experience would come in handy.

And it had.

Wildes was thriving, and Liam let me run absolutely rampant, full-tilt into any project I wanted to take on. It had all the things I loved about my old job, but none of the massive pressure. I was just an executive assistant, after all.

Whatever squeeze I was feeling around work was absolutely my own doing, and I was mature enough to understand that. But when these deals were closed, and we had a little more money—and a few more investors—in our pockets, I'd scale back. I swore it to myself. I'd fetch coffee and arrange meetings, and Cheryl would be thoughtfully reassigned under Ben's purview, and everything would be perfect.

"I promise, on Louboutins and champagne and everything I hold holy, Liam hasn't set foot in the club in at least six months. He won't be a problem."

Whitney sounded so sure, and that should have been a relief. Instead, I couldn't help but feel the little kernel of disappointment that pushed against my chest. Because the thought of Liam and me, at Dragon...together?

I shook my head. That was just a pipe dream, and a silly one, at that. I liked what I had with Liam. I didn't want it to change. Really.

My fantasy morphed, shifting into a faceless man in a suit and tie, petting me while I sat at his feet, doing my thinking for me, seeing to my comfort. Maybe with a flogger, seeing to my *dis*comfort.

My heart raced. Whitney was right. It had been too long since I'd last played. I was craving a scene. The mindless, enthralled bliss of handing all my trust and decisions over to another person. *That's* what I needed. Complete surrender.

"Let's do it."

"Really?" Whit squealed, bouncing on the cushions and setting Winston's tail wagging.

"Yeah. You're right. I need to let off some steam."

"Hell yes, you do! You deserve this. Wait, what are you going to wear? Come on." Whitney snapped her fingers, and Winston launched to his feet, kicking me in the stomach as he followed obediently. I smiled as I rose, following closely behind. Obediently.

***

Whitney winked from behind the bar while I observed the rest of the lounge. Dragon was, in a word, massive, with multiple stories, rooms, hallways, and dungeons that would make anyone want to stay and explore awhile.

Beyond the bar, the main floor of the lounge was one giant, sunken conversation pit, with clusters of plush chairs and gleaming wooden tables scattered throughout. Everything from the high-pile burgundy carpet to the low, understated but elegant light fixtures screamed class and money and...sex.

There were hints everywhere, subtle markers of what this club was really for. Wrought iron hooks spaced across the walls. The tempting red silk curtain that hid the hall of private rooms from view. The platform—stage really —in the middle of the room that would provide members with the perfect vantage point for viewing a demonstration.

Couples and groups sat together or alone, chatting or...not. In the corner, a woman sat with her sub perched, perfectly still, at her feet. At the bar, two Doms casually twirled the leashes of two men and a woman, a veritable pack of subs. Looked fun.

"Now that you've had the tour, we can discuss what you're looking for. Come along with me," Mistress Giselle crooked her fingers. I wasn't sure what I'd done to warrant a personal tour from Dragon's owner, but the club was known for its high level of service. Maybe this was just part of the package.

She led me to the front of the club where the main offices and rooms for Dom/sub meetings and interviews took place. She swayed ahead without looking back, certain I'd follow. She wasn't wrong.

It may have been a long time since I played a scene, but my training was still strongly ingrained. I knew how and when to yield to a master, or mistress as the case may be. Besides, I could feel the attention of the room on me. I was fresh meat, and I felt like it. I lowered my eyes, following in silence, feeling like every step was an interview.

Was there someone here tonight who might want to play with me? Were they watching right now? The thought sped my heart, and I felt a flutter between my legs. It really *had* been a long time.

"I usually like to wait a few visits before I try to match someone, get to know them, so to speak," Mistress Giselle gestured to a high-backed chair in her office. The rich, purple brocade pattern matched the paper on the walls. Lucite furniture clustered around a tall fireplace, and her massive iron desk stood demandingly in the center of the room. She settled behind it like a feather on a placid lake.

"However, I've had an intriguing opportunity pop up, and I find I can't help myself. Would you indulge me?"

"Yes, Ma'am." The offices and meeting rooms were strictly for introductions and negotiations. Everyone was equal here, which meant I didn't have to lower my eyes, but I wanted to. Everything about Mistress Giselle, from her blood-red lips to her warm, ebony skin, commanded attention. The high tilt of her chin screamed control and competence, and every part of my little submissive soul wanted to bow down at her feet and ask her to please, please take very good care of me. Her lips tilted like she knew it, too.

"It's an interesting proposition. You come highly recommended. Very highly, Ava," she repeated, tapping a razor-sharp, emerald green nail on the file that sat on the table between us. "But you mentioned you're not looking for a full D/s relationship commitment at this time. You have someone at home, perhaps?" No judgement in the question, just curiosity. Like she'd seen that kind of arrangement before.

"No, Ma'am. Just...work takes up a lot of my focus right now."

"I see," she smirked, eyes twinkling. "Well, you're not a brat, which narrows down your matches quite a bit. And you're open to many new experiences, but your favorite play involves power exchange."

Why was my mouth suddenly dry? Was that bad? No. I'd been taught early, thankfully, by a good Dom, that none of my sexual cravings were bad.

"Yes, Ma'am."

"Oh, you are very polite, aren't you? I have a member who's rather experienced, strong hand, mostly focused on power dynamics as well. Glowing reviews from previous subs." Her eyes narrowed, considering. "And he's looking for a partner tonight. One night only."

"Oh." *Oh*. So...he sounded...perfect? Mistress Giselle was still skewering me with that appraising look of hers, and I wasn't sure what I was missing.

She hummed, eyes skating across my face, from my hairline to my neck. "I'm not so sure. He usually keeps his subs on a longer-term basis. He parted amicably with his last, but they were paired for nearly three years. Understanding that's his usual modus operandi, would you still be interested in meeting him?"

My breath sped, coming out in short pants. Three years? That was basically as long as I'd been in the game. A frisson of excitement ran down my spine, landing between my legs. He was really, really experienced then. The kind of Dom who would know exactly what to do to quiet the hamster wheel of my brain. To turn off that incessant gnawing anxiety that never left and help me find that perfect, floating place where nothing could touch me.

"I'm interested." I sounded breathy, and Mistress Giselle practically beamed down at me.

"Excellent. Why don't you follow me, and we'll get you situated in a meeting room."

She showed me to a small room off the front hallway, its walls painted a dark, sultry green. The plain wooden table and chairs were painted black, shiny under the dim recessed lights. A cabinet stood in the corner with a pitcher of water and exquisitely cut crystal glasses.

"I'll show him right in and leave the two of you to get acquainted without me. You're under no obligation to, obviously, but some subs like to assume a nice position. Give the Doms a taste of what they can expect."

As soon as the door clicked closed, I fell to my knees. The hand-scraped wooden floors were hard under my skin, but it felt like home to me. I bid my heart to still its racing, bowing my head. Waiting.

The next person to walk through that door might be someone who would dominate me. Take care of me. I needed to thank Whitney properly later. I hadn't realized how much I wanted this, needed it, until right at that moment, with the shivering excitement of potential humming under my skin like an electric current.

The door opened and heavy, confident footfalls echoed through the room, then everything was quiet.

Chapter 4
Liam

"Liam."

"Mistress Giselle." I saluted her with my whiskey. "Can I buy you a drink?"

Her laugh was sultry, shivering in the air between us. "It's the least you could do. You've sent my staff into an absolute tizzy." She clicked her tongue at me, reaching for a flute of champagne the bartender was already passing across the counter. At Dragon, Giselle was the king and the rest of us mere servants. Or peasants. Or prisoners. Whatever suited her fancy from night to night.

"I told Andrew not to worry about it." The host at the front desk had nearly swallowed his tongue when I'd shown up and requested a sub for the night. "If no one's around that matches my profile, I'll have a few drinks and go home." Maybe that was for the best. There was a reason I'd avoided this place for so long. No matter how much fun I had, I couldn't truly relax into my scenes. It all felt wrong somehow. Off. My former sub, Laura, had been understanding and, by all accounts, was now enjoying a fantastic match with another Dom, courtesy of Giselle, of course.

"Well, that's the issue, dear Liam. We actually do have a match for you tonight. Beautiful, well-trained. Highly recommended. Mostly interested in power play."

So, my ideal partner. "What's the catch?"

"It's her first night."

"Come on."

"Just consider it for a moment," she tried to persuade me, but I wasn't interested.

"I don't want to train anyone, G. I need someone solid for one night. That's it."

Her eyes narrowed, and I resisted the urge to take a step back. "Do me, the woman with decades of experience matching players together, the courtesy of at least looking at her file before you insult me without thinking."

"I apologize." She smacked a folder into my hand. It was thin, very thin. I nearly commented on it, but a single withering look from G held my tongue.

I flipped through the anonymized papers. Health records, kink preferences. A three-two-one list of things she liked and her limits. One being a hard limit, three being the things I could do that would send her to the moon. I scanned the pages. "Huh."

"That's what I thought. Not every day I find such compatibility. Check her references, Liam."

Also anonymized, they were effusive, praising this woman's poise, her craving for submission. Her willingness to serve.

My cock stirred. That sounded right up my alley. Actually, the more I read, the more she seemed...perfect.

"She's not interested in taking on a full relationship. Says work is pretty intense right now." Giselle sipped her wine.

"Is she willing to meet?"

"She's waiting in one of the meeting rooms as we speak. When I mentioned your depth of experience, she practically started salivating."

I only hesitated for a moment longer, scanning her list again, picking out the things that turned her on most—power exchange, flogging, toys. Punishment. My mind was already spinning through scenarios that would please her. Make her beg and cry and make me feel...in control.

The thought tasted sweet. Usually, I felt like I was carrying the weight of the whole damn world. These deals, the revenue, the investors—they all buzzed around me, a constant rotation of uncontrollable variables and expectations I couldn't manage. Here though, that all changed.

I was lord and master, and I knew exactly what to do. I didn't worry about business deals or revenue or, God willing, the inconvenient thoughts of Ava Anderson that entered my head every time I had a woman stretched out underneath me.

It had been long enough now, and I'd probably gotten over that particularly bad habit. I had just needed a little break, a chance to retrain my brain to *not* think about long, silky black hair and sharp green cat eyes every time I was paddling someone, or balls-deep inside them. "Let's see her, then."

As I followed G to the meeting rooms, a familiar lightness overtook my body, the awareness that came with knowing I was about to be obeyed.

Madame gestured to a door. "I know I don't have to remind you of the cameras we have in these front rooms. Meetings are unchaperoned, but I won't stand for intimidation or abuse."

I inclined my head. "Of course not. You know me."

"I do." She grinned, looking a little like the cat who got the cream, patting my cheek fondly. "And I have no worries at all. In fact, I think I'll be on the edge of my seat seeing how this will work out." She gave me a final, almost-smacking pat before she turned on her heel and swayed down the hall.

I took a breath as I opened the door. My brain short-circuited. My only thought was that my highest, most fantastical expectations could never have matched the vision in front of me.

Ava Anderson. On her knees. For me.

My half-mast dick roared to attention, blood pulsing to my cock so fast I was dizzy. Or maybe I was just brought low, or high, or to a new fucking realm of existence looking at Ava like this. Knowing...

I turned, but Giselle was already gone. I looked back at the file in my hand. *This* was Ava? Those kinks, the flogging, the power-play. Finally, my attention settled back on her as if ensnared. I wasn't willing to look anywhere else for more than a second.

Ava, *my* Ava. My secretary, my business partner, my best friend, kneeling on the cold wooden floor clad only in a nearly sheer, lace-trimmed slip. The ivory color was stark against her skin, and even with the heavy shadows of the dim room, I could make out every curve of her body. Hips, ribs, breasts.

I'd never in my wildest dreams could have imagined that Ava ball-busting Anderson would be into submission, but the proof of it was in my hand, and right in front of my face. It sent a streak of desire and heady, possessive power straight through my veins.

I let the door close behind me. She didn't so much as flinch, her eyes still on the floor, unaware of who stood in front of her. Even after I took a full minute to gather my thoughts, she hadn't so much as lifted her eyes to try to sneak a peek. She was good, which shouldn't have been a surprise. Ava excelled at everything she did.

Her deference tightened my cock even more as I considered all the ways she anticipated my needs at work. She bent and swayed around my high-handed, no bullshit style and...and *served* me. Well.

I cleared my throat. The reminder of work flooded my brain with the impossibility of this situation. Sense finally set in. "Ava."

A reaction this time, a light jerk of her shoulders. Anyone could have missed it, anyone other than me, a man who damn near made a study of this woman every single day. A man trained to watch every little twitch and flutter of his subs, and she could...she could be my...

"Look at me." I commanded again when she didn't move. Damn, she was good, holding the posture even though I knew she recognized my voice and was probably as off-kilter as I was. *Perfect.*

Her head rose, light flowing across her sleek hair, gathered at the back of her neck in a low ponytail I could take in my fist and...

"Did you know I'd be here tonight?" I had to ask, because in some crazy, alternate universe off-chance that she had known, that she was here like this for me...I would take it.

"No." She paused, stiffening a degree before she added, "Sir."

Our eyes locked, and I could see the moment she realized the effect the word had on me. It was like a blow.

"You should stand up. This isn't...we're not doing this." I sounded harsher than I intended, but I needed to yank the emergency brake on my runaway thoughts. Seeing her like this was too tempting, too close to fantasies I'd never allowed myself to imagine. I turned on my heel as she stood, graceful and fluid.

"I swear I didn't know you'd be here. I avoid Dragon for that reason."

My hand hovered over a pitcher of cool water, wishing it were scotch. I never drank when I was about to do a scene, and had promptly abandoned my whiskey back in the lounge at the thought of her, this sub who might make me forget my impossible attraction to my assistant.

Joke was on me, and there was no way I'd be playing tonight. Not with Ava, and not with anyone else. I had the fleeting, devastating thought that maybe now that I'd seen her here, like this, I'd never be able to play with anyone again.

"You knew I was a member here?"

"Yes." I knew her well enough to hear the implied "of course" layered underneath her words.

"You have me at a disadvantage. I didn't know you were into the scene." I filled two glasses and set them on the small wooden table in the center of the room.

"Well, you..." She glanced around like she wanted to escape.

"I what? Might as well tell me. Not many secrets left between us now."

Her eyes flickered to mine as she took a shaking sip, draining half her glass in a single pull. I wanted to tell her to stop avoiding my question, but now that we were sitting together, in this room, telling her what to do would cross a line I knew I'd never be able to come back from. She swallowed, face scrunching. "You're the one who got me into all this."

I nearly dropped the empty glass she pushed back into my hand, gripping just in time to keep the delicate tumbler from shattering on the floor. "What?"

"In my first few weeks at Wildes, I was in your wallet, getting a credit card to pay for a company expense. Your membership card fell out, and I did some Googling."

"And you liked what you saw?" I worked to keep my voice steady as I refilled her glass, this time with a slice of lemon from the sideboard.

"The idea of giving up control, of understanding exactly what I had to do to get something right, was appealing." Her face transformed as she spoke. I'd bet all the money in Wildes' accounts that being a sub was more than just appealing. That she loved it, craved it. My dick twitched against the seam of my pants. "I've been in the lifestyle ever since, mostly over at Eden. Since I knew you were...here."

I took a measured sip of my own drink. Eden. She'd been avoiding me, and this very interaction. Smart girl. I probably should be avoiding this interaction, too. "You come very highly recommended," I said instead, trying to sound nonchalant when in reality, I had no idea what I wanted. To leave? To stay? To beg her for a night? One, single...

"You do, too. Your subs like you."

"Your Doms think you hung the damn moon." At her blush, my heart melted in my chest. Ava got heated with anger, with adrenaline, maybe. But she never blushed. And now, at the slightest hint of praise, a flush of pink rose up her neck. I wanted to feel it, lay my hands where her blood rushed to her skin. I wanted to make her do it again.

I rolled my head across my shoulders, working out the stiffness and working hard to overcome the instincts I'd honed over the years of being a Dom to test her, work her to her limits. Her eyes lifted to mine again, green and sharp, but now I saw a new, untouched vulnerability there I wanted to protect with my life. Fuck it.

"You're exceptional, Ava." I told her she did good work all the time, thanked her for the attention she gave to projects, the damn paperwork she filed or whatever. This wasn't that. It was earnest, targeted praise from a Dom to a sub, and she knew it.

Pink worked its way to her cheeks, and her chest sank in a sigh. "Thank you." Her eyes lowered to her drink, her training taking over, too. It awoke something primal inside me, a roaring need in my chest. To protect her, claim her, serve *her*. I'd stop, I swore to myself I would, but I just needed...just a taste.

"If I told you to get on your knees right now, you would."

"Of course." She didn't lift her eyes, making it sound so easy. Simple. I commanded, she obeyed. The raw, foundational basis of any Dom/sub relationship.

But this wasn't easy, or simple. Not for us. I let her stare at the lemon floating in her water for a few more moments. If this standstill happened in a business meeting, my Ava, secret COO at Wildes Capital, would have gotten up and left by now, but I wasn't dealing with the woman I knew. Just like she wasn't dealing with the boss she was used to. We were strangers, in a way, and as liberating as that thought was, I couldn't follow it to its end. I wouldn't go there.

"Obviously, we can't do this."

"Right." Her throat bobbed, skin still touched with pink.

"Drink." She did, without thinking, and it was perfect. "Good." It left my mouth before I could stop it because it *felt* simple, and right. Maybe it was this place, this room. I was conditioned to be a Dom here.

Or maybe you're just meant to be her *Dom.*

Another fluttering sigh left her lips, and her eyes squeezed shut.

"Right." She stood, holding the cup out to me. "I think I should go."

I rolled the glass between my palms. "You don't want to stay for a drink?" I shouldn't have felt so desperate to keep her around, but I was in over my head here.

"I don't think that's a good idea." Her eyes met mine, and for a moment it was just me and her, like usual. Her lips tilted in a sad smirk. "Everything will be normal, right? On Monday?"

"Nothing that happens within these walls will have an impact on our work together. I swear to you, Ava." I hoped the vow would put her at ease, but her face tightened. She fiddled with the lacy hem of her slip. "What's wrong? Answer me," I ordered when she hesitated.

At my words, my tone, her spine snapped straight, eyes on the table in front of her. *So good*.

"I was just really looking forward to it."

Her words hit me like a weight, because she wasn't alone in that. "Me too. Been a hard week." Madame Giselle's words came back to me. Ava wasn't looking for a long-term partner right now because *work was intense*. Shit.

"Yeah," she sighed, her eyes drifting closed again. "I think I needed..." She trailed off, shrugging, still unable to meet my eyes even when they opened, and I got the feeling it wasn't because of her submissive training.

"You needed to give up some control. Take the pressure off for a few hours?" Her teeth sank into her lip. "Answer me."

"Yes." The *Sir* she didn't say, that we both wanted her to say, remained silent.

"Me too."

"You could still..." Her eyes flickered to the door, where Dragon and all its delights waited beyond. "If you wanted."

"I don't." Not anymore. "I can leave, and you can..." I looked at the door, too.

"I don't want to, either."

I fought for a breath, drowning in the open, uncovered reality of our desires, along with the unspoken understanding that if I couldn't be here with her, I didn't want to be here at all. And she felt the same.

Another moment dragged between us, my eyes darting across her body. The cream silk, the way her shoulders rose and lowered with her soft breaths. And I realized I was completely and absolutely screwed.

I reached for the folder I'd set on the table. "If we do this," I started. Her head lifted, nearly the most movement I'd seen from her all night. I reached into my lapel pocket. "*If* we do this, no sex," I commanded, to set her expectations, but mostly to keep my own fantasies from running wild all over her.

"Agreed." She sat back down.

"Would you...want to play tonight? Within some parameters?"

"Yes," she spoke before I'd even finished asking, her eagerness tightening my pants again. Damn, I shouldn't be doing this, shouldn't even be *thinking* about this. But my pen was already moving, scribbling over the back of a paper from her file.

"You want a scene, Precious?" The endearment slipped out before I could rein it in. I'd thought of her that way too many times. Precious, untouchable, pristine and priceless. But her irises blew, even as her head lowered.

"Yes, please, Sir." Ah, fuck, fuck, fuck. I couldn't say no to her, to that *please* that reached down my throat and grabbed my guts in a fist. The room was small, and I barely had to move to reach over and lift her chin up. Her eyes stayed down.

"When I lift your face, I want you to look at me. When I ask you a question, answer it honestly and immediately. You're not punished for your thoughts. I want them."

Her eyes snapped to mine. "Yes, Sir."

My thumb stroked her jaw. She was flawless, and I wanted to tell her so, to heap praise on her. Make her unequivocally aware of how much she made me want her. But damn, the scene hadn't even started yet, and she still needed to earn it.

I forced my hand and attention back to the paper as I kept writing. "No sex. What about touching?"

"Only the skin you can see. Nothing under the dress."

"I think dress is a generous word." My attention flickered over the nearly-sheer silk. "Semantics, I suppose. Kissing?"

She only thought for a few seconds. "Not on the mouth."

"Pretty Woman rules."

She smiled. "Exactly." My arm reached out again with a mind of its own, my finger swiping across her bottom lip.

"I like your smile. Don't hold it back if you like something." The corners of her lips pressed deeper under the pad of my finger.

"Yes, Sir."

"Good," I cleared my throat, attention back on the contract rapidly forming under the tip of my pen. She watched, too, as our rules became tangible. "Only power exchange tonight. Your safeword is papaya. Repeat that back to me."

I raised my head when she faltered, her brows folding into a frown.

"Do you really think we need a safeword for this?" She nodded at the contract.

"I think it's my job to make sure you feel safe and comfortable no matter what we do, and if I give you a safeword, you'll use it if you need to use it. Understood?"

Her throat cleared as she shifted in her chair. "Yes, Sir." Her eyes lowered.

"What's the safeword?"

"Papaya, Sir."

I scribbled a few more lines of our expectations. Our scene. My mind ran through the list of questions and key points I usually covered when I took a new sub. It had been a while, but I knew what to ask and tell to make a good partnership. But this was Ava, and I knew her better than I knew myself. She trusted me, and I trusted her, and that was, honestly, all that mattered.

"And..." She trailed off.

"And?" My pen hovered over the paper. Her swallow was loud enough to reach my ears.

"And what happens here, stays here. Just one night. On Monday, everything is back to normal."

I pushed away the pang of disappointment. "Of course." Of course this could only be one night. Even one night was too risky. I could feel her attention on me as I finished up the contract, sliding it across the table. She took the pen when I offered it.

"You're going to give me a cuddle?" She asked, reading over the detailed outline of what I would and would not do tonight. Her nose wrinkled adorably.

"If you're giving me your free will for the evening, the least I can do is give you a hug. Aftercare is important no matter how much or little we do."

"I see." Her eyes flickered across the paper, running down the list. I nearly held my breath as I watched intently, pinpointing the exact second she faltered.

"I welcome changes, if you have them," I prompted, her eyes noticeably stuck in one spot. More of that lovely flush spread across her forehead, but she hesitated. I tapped the pen lying inert between her fingers. "I mean that, Ava."

She hummed, glancing at the pen before crossing a line out, scribbling, then signing the sheet in her familiar, loopy signature. She held still while I pulled the contract towards me, her spine too straight, muscles rigid.

Hair ~~stroking~~ pulling

My fingertips drummed across her edit, heart picking up an extra beat or two. Damn. Damn, damn, damn it. This was a horrible, awful, unavoidably tempting idea. I hesitated.

"You want to put a limit on how hard I can pull?"

She sucked her bottom lip into her mouth at my question. "No, Sir. I trust you."

My signature sprawled across the paper, the contract folding neatly into thirds before I slid it into my pocket.

"As soon as we step out that door, we begin." Her fingers slid gracefully into my palm as I offered my hand to pull her to her feet. "Do you need to use the restroom before we start? Hungry or thirsty?"

She shook her head, even as her throat bobbed.

"Alright." She waited patiently by the door as I put the glasses in the sink for an attendant to clean later, then met her on the threshold of the room. I hesitated. I should say something. But what could you say when you were doing something like this, so foundationally world-rocking and, arguably, reckless with the person you trusted most? In the end, I didn't say anything at all as I stepped into the hallway.

She followed on my heels, also silent, and nothing had ever felt more right.

Chapter 5
Liam

Couples or groups gathered around the main lounge relaxing or playing subtle scenes. Here, a woman fed her sub a grape, tugging gently on his hair. There, a man sat facing a wall while his partner chatted with a few other members. Telltale streaks of a cane stood out on his smooth skin.

Most of the people here would split off over the course of the night to go home, or rent one of the private rooms in the back. Some would go at it like bunnies, and others would leave satisfied just knowing they could hold, or forfeit, power with a snap of their fingers.

It was a gilded dungeon. The classiest, most delicate stage that allowed us to give in to some of our basest desires.

And walking through the room with Ava on my heels—head down, exactly two steps behind me, as she'd been instructed—was heady. New subs always turned heads, and I could feel the gazes of other Doms as we walked across the room. Knowing she was mine, if only for tonight, raised my chin that much higher.

"Wildes!" Javier Morales waved me over to a cluster of low wing-back chairs across the room. I changed course in his direction, a surge of heat flickering through my veins when I knew without looking back that Ava would follow. It stoked higher when Javi's eyes widened for a half-second when he caught sight of her.

He stayed more on the venture capital side of things, but we'd crossed paths enough both inside and outside of Dragon to become friends.

Even though he wasn't one of my investors, he certainly knew who Ava was. She was usually standing right beside me at the fancy galas and dinners where I often encountered Javier outside of the club.

"Having fun?" he asked as we shook hands, a wicked gleam in his eye.

"Always." When I glanced back at Ava, my gut seized up at the sight of her. Shoulders back, proud, with her head bowed slightly. This wasn't a lowly, cowed slave. This was a woman who knowingly, willingly, and enthusiastically was handing her freedom to me on a silver platter. The sight sent a spark of fire roaring through my veins.

"Lovely to meet you, Wildes. I've been looking forward to this." The new voice made Ava's shoulders tense. I turned to greet the woman who had been sitting in a chair opposite Javi. I grasped her hand, brushing a kiss across her knuckles, cataloguing her face. "Andrea Smithson." Something tickled at my memory as she introduced herself, but try as I might, I couldn't place her.

Her silver-streaked blonde hair was pulled into a severe bun, and her dark, pointed eyeliner and red lips gave her a predatory look. Her floor-length leather duster nearly hid a black silk bustier and leather pants. A Domme, but not one I knew.

Andrea smirked as I tried to identify why her name was familiar. "I'm sure your associate can ring that particular bell for you, if you're at a loss."

My attention scraped over Ava once more. Her toes flexed in the carpet. She was probably about to levitate from the need to rescue me. She knew exactly who this woman was, and why she was important.

The need to tell me, to whisper it into my ear and smooth this awkward encounter over, was probably killing her.

Too bad.

"My associate isn't here to work tonight. We can ring our own bells, don't you think? Potential investor?" I took an educated guess. Whoever Smithson was, she had money written all over her.

"Potential," the woman agreed, settling back in her chair. "Your assistant has been courting me hard, teasing out possibly good news with VestedAI. My members would be interested to hear about that."

Smithson. The name finally clicked into place with her clue. "Of course. Andrea. Congratulations on the promotion." She'd recently been named chief investing officer of one of the largest pension funds in the northeast. Usually Wildes didn't go after players as big as her, but Ava had been adamant we needed to think bigger if we were going to grow as quickly as we wanted. She'd been right, of course, as she usually was.

"Hasn't been a walk in the park, let me tell you."

"The market has been all over the place," Javi chimed in. I left the two of them to bemoan stocks while I tended to Ava, skimming my hand down her arm. She was silky smooth, so soft I ran my fingers back up again.

Her eyes were locked on the carpet, muscles rigid, a far cry from the loose, relaxed way she'd followed me out of the meeting room.

My voice was low in the quiet room, only for her ears as the backs of my fingers stroked across the tendons that stood out in her neck. "Ms. Smithson isn't your concern tonight. I am."

"Yes, Sir." She tried to sound quiet and confident, but I caught the waver of unease threading through her voice. I grasped her jaw, holding tighter than was necessary, just shy of pinching. Her eyes widened.

"I expect your complete attention on me and the tasks I give you. Not work, not her. Not anything else." I looped my free hand through her long ponytail, pulling to force her gaze up, up, up, until I was staring straight down into those green cat eyes. "Andrea knows not to allow what happens within these walls to affect whatever deal you're trying to work out. And if she can't do that, well, then that's my problem to deal with. Isn't it?"

Her shoulders lowered, face relaxing. Even her head tilted further back in my hold. "Yes, Sir." That was better. That's what she needed—what we both did. Her to submit, to offer up her power. Me, to take it.

"Good. Go get me a drink. And breathe."

"Yes, Sir." She was beautiful as she turned back to the bar. She always had a poise about her, an aura of confidence. Seeing it now, in this context, drove me a little crazy. My fingers curled into fists as I willed myself not to reach for her.

Then again...if I only had one night with her like this, I'd do whatever the hell I wanted.

"Stop." She froze in her tracks, and I grabbed her hair again. Silk against my skin. I pulled it, jerked it, really. Harder. Her eyelids fluttered. Oh, that was lovely. "When you get back, I expect to know exactly how many breaths you took."

"Yes, Sir." Her brow furrowed for half a second before smoothing out. I ran my fingers through her hair one last time before releasing her.

"Drink. Now." I wanted to swat her ass, but that would be too close to spanking, and no matter how much I wanted to explore that avenue with her, it wasn't in the plan tonight.

"I didn't realize you two were partners outside of the firm," Javi commented. When I turned, both he and Andrea were watching Ava cross the room.

"We're not usually. Tonight is…probably a one-time thing."

"Shame," Andrea said, sipping her glass, her eyes raking up and down Ava's spine. "She's lovely."

"She is." I sat, not minding the other Domme's clear appraisal. That was the name of the game here, especially since half the members *wanted* to be seen as property, and the other half wanted to own. Pride surged as I pulled the small cushion from underneath my chair, perfectly designed for what I had in mind.

"And I know what I told her was true. Nothing that happens here will affect whatever deal you're working on with her."

When Andrea scoffed, spearing me with an offended look, I knew I didn't have anything to worry about. But I'd had to check. I'd promised Ava.

"I'm not a novice, Wildes. I can separate what happens here from what goes on out there." Andrea nodded toward the front of the building, where the rest of the city hustled while everything in this room seemed suspended. Untouchable. "If anything, it's nice to see. I was beginning to think your assistant was a robot. Good to know she has other things going on under the surface. If anything, it makes working with you two seem even more intriguing."

"Nice to know you're intrigued. Maybe we can talk about that during work hours next week?"

"Yes, yes," Andrea waved me off, rolling her eyes. I smirked. No wonder Ava liked her so much. "Message received. No work talk."

"Thank you." I rose as Ava made her way back to our table, because I was a goddamn gentleman, and I wanted to get the best view I possibly could for the next part.

"Scotch, neat, Sir." She offered the drink without taking her eyes off the carpet.

"You know me so well, I love it," I murmured, stroking the backs of my fingers down her arm again. Her lips twitched before lifting into a small, satisfied smile.

"Thank you, Sir."

"Do you have something to report to me?"

"I took seventy-eight breaths, Sir."

"Good. Kneel." I snapped my fingers at the cushion I'd placed a few inches from my chair, and she dropped to her knees. Yeah, that alone was worth the price of admission. I took a sip of my drink, studying her, walking to the side to view her from another angle. Gorgeous.

She'd sprung for the good scotch, too. What a good girl. I'd have to tell her again, soon.

"This is a lovely carpet, don't you think?" I bent, pulling her skirt evenly across her thighs, positioning her ankles so they wouldn't ache as badly. She shivered when my fingers dragged up the soft skin of her leg, goosebumps raising wherever I touched. So responsive. She bit her lip, concentrating on the carpet below us.

"Yes, Sir."

"I'd like you to appreciate it further." I grabbed her ponytail again, pulling enough to allow her to feel the tug on her scalp, just like she'd requested.

"Yes, Sir."

"Count the stars in the pattern."

"Alright, Sir."

It would be so easy to tip my mouth down to hers, to see if she tasted as sweet as I thought she would. I watched her throat work when my fingers tightened even more, her neck exposed to me. "And really count, pretty girl. Don't just identify the pattern and do the fancy mental math to extrapolate how many there are. I want your eyes on every. Single. One."

Her neck tilted an inch further, muscles going limp at the order, mind almost visibly emptying as I doled out her assignment.

"Yes, Sir." Her agreement was husky with pleasure as she focused on my command, not the potential investor watching us quietly, or the other members around the club.

Ava's sharp eyes went distant, a smile playing across her lush lips. I lowered my head, so close to kissing her, I could feel the slightest whisper of her skin directly underneath mine.

But we'd set the rules, and I really *was* a gentleman. I tilted my head sideways at the last second, pressing a lingering kiss on her cheekbone before settling into my chair and releasing her silky black-brown strands, leaving her to her work.

"If we're not supposed to talk about work, I don't know what we'll talk about at all," Andrea griped. I tore my eyes away from Ava's bowed form.

"Not mine, at least. Javi, what's going on in your world?"

Our conversation meandered. As always, Javi had a good eye for the newest tech startups that were actually worth a damn, and I enjoyed Andrea's dry humor.

But even though the conversation flowed around us, and the liquor was good, it barely held a quarter of my attention. All of my focus was consumed by the woman at my feet. With her head bowed, I allowed my gaze to linger—a luxury I never allowed myself in the office, where I was so very good about keeping my eyes and hands and thoughts on the right side of professional.

It was a relief just to look at her. Smooth skin, the pert, round outline of her breasts against the thin fabric of her gown. She was a lush landscape of toned muscle and flawless skin. She worked hard for that body, and damn if I didn't want to appreciate it while I had the opportunity.

I tuned in and out of the conversation, staring at Ava so hard she could probably feel me taking stock of every inch of her body. If she could, she didn't show it, though, eyes trained on the carpet, chest moving in slow, meditative draws of air. When I leaned forward to place my empty glass on the table, she didn't move.

"She's barely fidgeted since you put her on her knees," Javi observed after I placed another drink order with the waitress I beckoned. There was a hushed sort of reverence in his tone. And, yeah, that was part of the appeal of being a Dom. Showing her off, showing every person in this club just what she would do, just how far she'd go, to please me. I'd assumed she'd be good at this, but the longer she knelt perfectly still, studying the rug, the more I knew it in my bones.

"Some people are just made for this," Andrea echoed my own thoughts. "I can't believe this is her first night with you. Usually, they need to be trained up before they show this kind of discipline with someone new."

Even with the cushions, most subs only made it about twenty minutes before they needed to shift their weight around to ease the stiffness and tingling in their legs. I'd assumed Ava could make it for closer to thirty, because it was second nature to assume she'd excel at whatever task I gave her.

She'd made it nearly forty-five minutes, and I still hadn't seen the type of movement or adjustment that signaled a sub getting antsy or pained.

I wasn't sure if she was just that eager to please me, or if she was preoccupied. There were a lot of stars...

My hand stroked down her hair, the first contact I'd given her in nearly an hour, but I wanted to make sure she hadn't fallen into some crazy meditative hallucination. It wasn't uncommon to see a sub reach a higher plane of existence, but it usually took a lot more work from me than just telling them to kneel.

Her neck arched, leaning back lazily into my caress. Ah. She was there, just very, very, very good at concentrating. "She came to me already perfect."

A soft sigh breezed out of her lips, and her head tipped sideways until her cheek rested against my thigh. It was the type of unsanctioned move I'd usually punish a sub for—stealing contact without express permission—but when her eyes blinked open, gazing at me with soft, empty satisfaction, I couldn't help myself, stroking my fingers across her cheek. She blinked again, slow and sated, a smile curling her lips.

"Hi, pretty girl."

"Hi."

"Been busy?"

She sighed again, eyes heavy-lidded as she nodded. She looked warm and relaxed in a way I'd never seen her before.

"How many are there, precious?"

"Two thousand, five hundred and thirteen."

"You're sure." Not really a question, but I wouldn't be worth my salt if I just took her word for it.

"Yes, Sir."

"Such a good girl," I crooned, leaning down to run my nose across her cheekbone. She strained closer to me. Her trust, her obvious pleasure, the way she arched into my touch—all of it went straight to my dick. My fingers skimmed across her throat. I wanted to grab her jaw and cover her mouth with mine, thrust my tongue inside and *own* her, show her what it did to me when she was so, so good...

Dangerous, a voice in my head warned. Then again, this whole night was dangerous. But still, I heeded it. She trusted me to honor our boundaries, not dry hump her on the rug.

I pressed a soft kiss to her temple, a mere shadow of what I actually wanted to do with her. "Good girls get rewarded, don't they?"

"Yes, Sir."

"Come here." She'd earned it, and I barely had to tug on her arm. She came willingly into my lap like she'd been looking forward to it for hours. I draped her across me, ass on my thigh, legs folded across the arm of my chair. "You did so well, Ava. Perfectly."

She hummed, contented as she tucked her forehead against my neck, nearly collapsing against me while I rubbed her knees, her sore calves, paying special attention to the areas I knew would have gone numb, the places flooding with blood, probably tingling and stinging as a result of her submissive position.

Ava Anderson, kneeling at my feet and then melting in my arms. My cock throbbed against her ass, and I knew she felt it. I'd been hard as a damn rock ever since I'd opened that meeting room door.

She only tucked herself closer, the movement sending her hips into mine so subtly, it might have been an accident. But Ava didn't do accidents. I grasped her thigh, squeezing the soft skin there just enough to get her attention, not to bruise. "Careful, Ava. Don't take what I don't offer."

"Yes, Sir." Her response was prompt, contrite, and would have been exceptional, just like the rest of her performance tonight, except for the small smile she hid against my throat. "I'm sorry, Sir."

Damn, I should have punished her for that, too, but it was getting late, and she felt good in my lap. And, perhaps, possibly, just maybe, I was a pushover when it came to my assistant.

"I'm willing to overlook it for now. You looked so good at my feet. Here," I picked up the martini glass the server had quietly placed on the table next to my chair. Ava's favorite fancy vodka, shaken and dirty, just how she liked it. "Hands behind your back, gorgeous."

I usually wasn't so liberal with my praise, especially with a new sub. But, Christ, how could I not give them up with almost every breath when her hands linked behind her in seconds, lowered eyes just waiting to fulfill my every whim.

"Drink. Don't spill."

She sipped, craning her neck a bit to catch the liquid from the glass I held to her lips. I gave her another sip, watching the muscles in her neck work as she swallowed. Peering at her as I put the glass down.

"Open." I pulled an olive off the metal skewer, everything below my belt tightening to near pain when her lips parted to receive it. "Eat." I placed the olive between her teeth, nose skimming the delicate curve of her ear.

On the other side of the table, Javier and Andrea continued to chat, but I couldn't care less, my sole focus on the woman in my arms. When the olives were gone, her tongue darted out to taste the salt, the perfect pink against her pouty lips...

I rolled my hips. Just once, I swore. Just one time to feel her. Her soft ass pressed into my hard flesh, the perfect pressure. She'd feel like heaven wrapped around me.

A glint of white teeth in the dim room. She burrowed against my neck, arching her back until I ran my palm down her spine, stilling her, enjoying the feel of silk-covered muscle under my hands. "Enough now."

She sank into me, letting me hold her as I continued to rub sore legs.

But that was all. Because I wouldn't break my promises to Ava. Only my promises to myself. The ones I'd sworn years ago, to never think of her this way. The vows I'd kept until tonight.

Later, after I'd tucked Ava into a town car, I drove like a bat out of hell back to my brownstone and jacked off in the shower like a horny teenager.

And prayed that I could forget about this over the weekend. Because that was another promise I'd made her: that everything would go back to normal on Monday morning.

And I always kept promises to my subs.

I lay awake, haunted by the feeling of her pressing into my cock, knowing that for the first time in my life, I was playing a losing game.

Chapter 6
Ava

"Why do you have two coffees?" I demanded, stopping in the middle of the sidewalk. Winston's leash went taut as he lunged toward Liam.

"You're not supposed to yank her around," my boss admonished my wagging dog, sounding completely fine.

Except nothing was fine. I'd woken up Saturday feeling rested and relaxed and *wanting more,* which was not part of the plan.

I'd spent the last forty-eight hours promising myself that no matter how good Liam's skin had felt on mine, no matter how clearly I could still feel his obvious arousal under my thighs, that it was a one-time thing. Just one night to take the edge off, and everything would be fine now, normal. As promised.

As. Contractually. Obligated.

But now here he was, striding towards me with a drink carrier in his hand, two coffees nestled inside. Just like me.

"Why. Do you have. Two. Coffees?' I gritted, trying not to shiver when he took hold of my elbow to get me moving again. That was a normal touch, right? He'd grasped my arm before, right? Oh, God, this was *not* normal.

"One's yours."

"Mine?" My heart shot to my throat, racing as he gently nudged me toward the gates lining his brownstone's front steps. I dug my feet in. "I'm *your* assistant. I bring *you* coffee, not the other way around." I accused, sounding like he'd just rear-ended my car instead of bringing me caffeine.

"I know, but just today—"

"You said we'd be normal. This is not normal, Liam," I hissed, wrenching my arm away from his.

"I understand, bu—"

"Obviously not, because this is *not* normal and now we're just two assholes standing on the sidewalk with four cups of coffee." It was ridiculous how panicked I felt, but I couldn't help it. If I couldn't count on Liam to hold the line of professionalism we'd always kept between us, we were doomed. I didn't have the time or mental bandwidth or any damn *conviction* to maintain boundaries with the man who'd given me a glimpse of absolute kink heaven just two days ago. "Throw yours away."

He reared back. "No. You throw yours away."

"Absolutely not," I snapped with enough fire for Winston to whine at my feet. He was conflict-averse. "You're the one with the abnormal coffee. I got up at my *normal* time and went to the *normal* place because I'm being *normal*, as agreed. *You* are up early, with extra coffee. Not normal."

Liam's eyebrow quirked as I ranted, unimpressed. When I stopped to glare at him, he turned the cup in the cardboard holder he carried, flashing me the white logo on the side.

"That's..."

"Your favorite coffee place way too far away? Yes. But when it's my assistant's three-year work anniversary, I think it's worth waking up a bit early for."

"Oh."

"There's also a sizeable bonus check in your bank account by now, because that's what bosses do for the best assistant they've ever had."

"Oh." This *oh* was noticeably quieter than the last. He pulled one of the coffees out of his carrier, wafting the cinnamon scent of my favorite specialty latte right into my face. He removed the tray from my hands as I blankly took the cup from his.

"Let's save these for later. Or is four coffees between two assholes still too *abnormal* for you?" He smirked, and if I were a little further removed from the situation, I would have, too. I was the one being weird. He was being his usual charming, thoughtful self, and...I had to stop wigging out. He said he'd be normal, so we'd be normal.

I repeated the thought in my head over and over as he let us into his brownstone. Liam felt about Mondays the way vampires felt about the sun, so the whole office usually took the first day of the week from home. As closely as Liam and I worked, we got more done together than we did apart, and it hadn't taken long until I had my own desk in his home office, right next to his.

Winston fielded a treat Liam tossed him, then trotted over to settle on the dog bed Liam kept in the front room.

Was *that* normal? As I followed him through his entryway into the open-concept kitchen and main living area, I wondered if he and I had surpassed normal a long time ago, and it had taken some light hair pulling for me to realize it. My scalp tingled.

"Here." A wrapped breakfast sandwich landed on the granite of the island between us.

"Is this the spinach and bacon one?"

"Obviously." He didn't look up, rummaging in the bag for his own breakfast. My heart melted a little when he pulled out two containers of extra salsa, the exact way I usually ordered my favorite breakfast sandwich. He was a good guy and coworker and, yeah, so he knew my breakfast order, I knew his too, and that was *normal*, right?

"Thank you." I reached for the sandwich, simultaneously trying to grasp at some sense of equilibrium. I could be normal, even though everything inside me was pulling toward him, screaming for me to wrap myself around his body, attach to him like a barnacle and—

His hand whipped out, pinning a corner of the sandwich's wax paper to his countertop. I jolted at the sudden movement, jerking my eyes from the food to his face, but his attention stayed trained on the lid of his coffee.

"Ava." Something about his voice, the low tremor underneath his calm tone, tensed my shoulders.

"Yes?"

"As long as we're being abnormal, for just one moment longer?"

I waited, but he did, too. Like he was asking permission. A shiver snaked through my stomach, fluttery and uncertain and hopeful.

"Yes?" I didn't even know what I was agreeing to, but there was no doubt in my mind I wanted it. When it came to Liam, I wanted all of it.

"You are the best. That I've ever had."

Oh. Oh, God.

Heat flooded me, and everything between my legs tightened because he wasn't talking about me being his assistant. I sucked in a breath, held it when a smile threatened to break across my face. I stared down at his coffee just as intently as he did. When I finally had control, I let the air out of my lungs, the tension between us humming and expectant.

"Thank you. You were, too."

His head jerked in a nod, and his hand released the sandwich. In seconds, he'd disappeared up the stairs, probably to grab his laptop.

I gave in to the impulse to flatten myself on his counter. The rock was cool and grounding under my cheek, and I was so irrevocably in love with my boss, and nothing, *nothing* was normal.

Chapter 7

Ava

"I'm getting out of here before another crisis pops up. You remember what it was like to have free time?" Ben stood, gathering his laptop and folders from where they were scattered around the conference room table. Outside the glass walls, most of the cubicles were empty. Six p.m. on a Friday was usually a dead zone, but people had scrammed faster than usual this week. It had been a tough one, and they deserved it.

"No," Liam and I chimed. I avoided his gaze.

One of the longest, most frustrating weeks of my life, and it was only partially because I hadn't been able to carry on a normal conversation with my boss since last Friday. The due diligence for VestedAI was going to hell. One of the buyers for another company was getting greedy with his stipulations, and another was getting cold feet, questioning the valuation we'd agreed on months ago.

Oh, and our annual partner dinner was next week, and we still hadn't finalized the menu with our last-minute caterer. Oh, and all the other stuff we had to do to keep the company running.

Now would have been a great time to be able to look our CEO in the eye, but as the week had stretched on, it hadn't gotten any easier to convince myself I could go back to the way things were before.

I couldn't stop thinking about our night together, or move past the riot of emotions that kicked up when I thought about how he'd found the best ways to get me out of my head. How his fingers felt tugging on my hair.

And worse, I was completely clueless as to what Liam was thinking. Aside from his comment on Monday, he was cool and collected. His usual self.

In comparison, I was a twisting hurricane of raging heat and hormones, and it pissed me off. I'd become increasingly edgy and snappish all week long, feeling like I was drowning, not knowing if he was thinking about me. Pissed that I cared so much. Hurt that he seemed so fine.

"I miss my family," Ben continued. "All this fire drill bullshit better be done soon."

Liam barely grunted without glancing up from his screen. He'd hardly looked my way this week. At least, not that I had seen, and I'd been sneaking glances at him every chance I could. Was he really focusing on work, or was he masking like I was?

"Tell me about it. I don't remember the last time I saw the inside of my yoga studio."

I regretted the words almost instantly when Liam's attention whipped to me.

"You're not doing your yoga?"

My jaw clenched. What a rookie mistake. If I weren't so distracted, I'd never have admitted something like that in front of him. "Don't start with me."

His eyes narrowed. "I'll start whatever I want. Part of the deal of working here is that you take care of yourse—"

"Oh, look, it's Wesley. Come on in, Wes," I waved him in through the glass, ruthlessly cutting Liam off. His mouth snapped shut just like I knew it would. He never fought with me in front of the staff.

"They can substitute the appetizer you requested, but they'll have to prep it offsite so we don't cross-contaminate because of Johanson's shellfish allergy." Wesley started monologuing before the door was fully open, already holding a menu out for my perusal.

Liam got to it first, snatching it out of the air. His already irritated face transformed into something closer to a scowl as he read. "Why are you giving this to my assistant?"

At his sharp, proprietary tone, Wesley's eyes went wide. "Um, she's making final decisions on the menu for the partners' dinner."

"The fuck she is."

Wesley flinched as Liam dropped the menu on the table.

"Liam," I warned, glaring.

"Ava," he bit back at me. "No wonder you don't have time for yoga. You're doing asinine shit below your pay grade."

"I'm in charge of the partners' dinner."

"You are *managing* the partners' dinner. *He* is in charge. What's the point of having an event coordinator if he can't coordinate events?"

"Liam!" I stood, feeling the need to protect poor Wesley, who was glancing between the two of us in horror. So much for not arguing in front of the staff.

He shoved the menu back across the table in Wesley's direction. "It's food. Pick some."

"O-of course. Sorry, sir. And Ava, sorry, I..." Wesley backed out of the room, looking like he was in imminent danger of either being fired or punched in the jaw.

"That was ridiculously inappropriate," I started as soon as the door closed, watching Wesley scurry across the mostly deserted office floor.

"You taking on HR duties now, too? Going to write me up?" Liam shoved to his feet, mirroring me. "Ava, just because you *can* do everything doesn't mean you should."

"I delegate plenty."

"What's Cheryl working on these days?"

My mouth opened to fire back that Cheryl was plenty busy and if Liam was so concerned about her, maybe he should make her his primary assistant instead of me. Thankfully, Ben butted in before the words could fire out of me.

"Hey Mom? Dad? You know the kiddos get antsy when you fight." Ben nodded his head to the glass windows where Wesley was huddled in the elevator, whispering to someone from the marketing team as the doors closed. They were both eyeing us with worried looks. "I don't know what's been going on with you two this week, but something's weird. Figure it out before Monday."

Liam and I stewed in the ominous silence Ben left behind as he grabbed his bag and headed for the elevators. The air in the conference room felt stuffy, and I realized we were both standing, arms braced on the table like we were about to throw down.

His eyes crawled over my face, and I could feel it heat, blushing. Since Monday, we'd managed to avoid being trapped like this together, just the two of us without Ben or a client to buffer all the weird new feelings and unspoken words between us. Or maybe it was just me who'd gotten good at it, because I hadn't noticed anything different or off about Liam this week.

Though maybe, just maybe, now that we were alone, he'd—

"Have a nice night, Ava."

Then he was gone. I stood for several long moments, watching his back as he walked towards his office, dialing his phone. No dressing down. No admonishment for arguing with him in front of our colleagues.

Just...normal.

I sat back down, torn between the urge to crawl under the table or run after him, demanding to know what he was thinking. He obviously wasn't obsessing about our night together as much as I was. I was tied up in frickin' knots about it, and not in the fun way.

It was stupid, really. We hadn't had a very involved scene, but he'd been...perfect, and my head had emptied in blissful, meditative silence. Now that I'd had it with him, I wasn't sure it could ever be as good with anyone else.

And where that left me, I wasn't sure.

When my phone rang, I picked it up without looking at the number, grateful for the distraction. "Hello?"

"Ava?"

I jerked upright in my chair. "Mistress Giselle?"

"Hello, lovely. Do you have a moment?"

"Yes, Ma'am." Because what else could you say to the city's foremost Domme when she called your personal cell phone?

"Such good manners, even on the phone. I wanted to personally inform you that your membership dues have been paid through next year. Anonymously, of course."

My hand shot out to steady me against the table, feeling suddenly lightheaded and wobbly, even though I was sitting. "Ma'am?"

"Yes, yes, very generous. I was told in no uncertain terms to relay to you, vehemently, that the payment of your dues comes with no strings attached. Zero expectations of your beginning a partnership with this...anonymous individual. And I know I don't have to remind you that we don't tolerate any sort of coercion in the club. If you feel this is a manipulation, you tell me and I'll take care of it, understand?"

"Yes, Ma'am. It's...it's not." My eyes scanned the empty office, finding Liam's broad shoulders as he strode to the elevator bank. Confident. A king in his castle.

"I thought not, but I always have to check. We'll have your membership card ready tonight, if you'd like to come pick it up."

Liam entered the elevator, turning to face me as he pressed the button. Our eyes met, and I wasn't sure what he saw on my face, my expression, but his mouth quirked in a smirk, eyes hot and dark.

"Yes, Ma'am. I'll be there tonight."

Just before the doors closed, Liam's lips lifted into a full grin, as if he could hear me.

***

Dragon was just as breathtaking as it had been last week, but I moved through the rooms with purpose, one goal in mind.

Him.

He was sitting with a group of people close to the cluster of chairs we'd settled in last week. He was already watching, tracking me across the room while he took a lazy pull of his drink. It looked like sparkling water. No alcohol tonight.

Did that mean he wanted to do a more intricate scene? The nerves that had started fluttering when Mistress Giselle called me suddenly rioted. Maybe he hadn't meant for me to come back to him? Maybe my dues payment was just a gesture, like the breakfast sandwich on Monday?

He rose, fluid and confident. Still the king, just a different castle. When he gestured to me with two crooked fingers, the relief made my joints weak. I headed straight towards him, as if he already had me on a leash and only had to tug me closer.

"Ava." His voice thrummed across my skin, sending shivers between my legs.

"Sir."

"I have no expectations. You're free to be here with anyone. Doesn't have to be me, understand?"

"Yes, Sir." I floated to my knees, my submission before him a statement. As a sub, I knew my power—to choose who I submitted to and how. I was handing it over to him on a silver platter.

He hummed, hands stroking across my hair, pulled back in a ponytail again. "You don't want anyone else?"

"No, Sir."

"Good. Me neither."

Pleasure, *relief,* soared through me at his words. It wasn't just me. He felt it too. He sounded growly and possessive, fingers turning firm as he gripped my hair so hard I rose an inch. So good. "Because we have some things to work on, you and I. We need more ground rules if we're going to do this."

"Yes, Sir." Yes, please. Anything to keep his hands on me, his attention.

"And we need to address the fact that you've been a goddamned brat all week. You're better than that, Ava, and we both know it."

"I'm sorry."

"I'm sure you are. I assume you'll do better with more rules. Structure. Right?"

I'd been dangling on the edge of desire and uncertainty all week long, but he was offering me what I really needed. No more guessing. Black and white, right and wrong. Clear definitions of what we were at work, and outside of the office.

What would happen if something went wrong and all this blew up in our faces? My head dipped lower. That was his job now. He was already thinking about that, I was sure. Already had a plan that we'd lay out on ink and paper.

All the worry and anxiety of this week dripped out of my brain like honey.

"Yes, Sir."

"We'll discuss our rules of engagement, and you'll take your punishment like a good girl. After I finish my drink."

"Yes, Sir."

He sat, leaving me where I was. No cushion this time, which was probably for the best. Part of the punishment he had in mind for my attitude all week long.

But I didn't care. Punishment, I understood. Craved, even. Exact, consistent consequences so I'd know what would happen if I messed something up. He settled back into conversation with the people around us, but I paid them little mind. My attention was on the carpet, absorbed by the sound of his voice and the way his hands played across my hair, my shoulders, stroking and kneading.

It felt right. My thighs clenched, trying to hold back the arousal that was already coursing through me. Across the room, soft, but just loud enough to be heard over the music, there was a slight smack of flesh and the high-pitched groan of a sub who loved it and hated it at the same time.

Chapter 8
Liam

"I know you don't enjoy degradation, so this is about as close as I'll get with you." The papers in my hand landed on the table with a *snap*. "What the fuck, Ava?"

Ava startled where she sat in one of the black chairs in the same meeting room where all this started last week. She thought she'd gotten a taste of what I was like as a Dom? After just a little hair pulling?

There was a reason I didn't have to look too hard if I wanted a new partner. I was damn good at what I did, and she had crossed a line we'd agreed on, as well as several foundational boundaries to our community.

If she thought I was just going to let this week slide, she was in for a rude awakening.

"I'm sorry, Si—"

"I'm not Sir in here. And I didn't ask for an apology, I asked for an explanation for why you've been a damned pain in my ass all week."

Her satisfied smile from the lounge was gone now as I finally let loose some of the anger, the fear, that roiled through my veins, letting her see just how pissed I was. Her head lowered

"I know we said we'd act normal on Monday, but I couldn't..." she swallowed, forehead pinching in frustration. "I wasn't sure what you were thinking—"

"And you didn't think to ask?" My voice was low, calm. Danger-ously so. There were a few things in life I could depend on. Death, taxes, Ava telling me what was on her mind. She'd let me down. And scared the shit out of me.

Her brows snapped into a frown. "It's not like you were offering up your thoughts on the matter. You seemed fine! *Normal*." She looked like the word tasted bitter on her tongue, some of that snark from this week peeking out.

I braced on the table, leaning forward to grip her jaw, forcing her to look at me. "I am your *boss*, Ava. I can't pause a meeting to ask if your attitude would improve with a good spanking." Not that I hadn't thought about it multiple times over the last few days. In hindsight, maybe I should have, but I was too concerned that her frustration towards me was really regret.

"I'm not your Dom out there. I can't make decisions for you or take control. I'm not a mind reader, either," I continued, watching the muscles in her neck and shoulders tighten. I was sick of the days of tension between us, and I didn't care how wound up she got, I wanted this out in the open. "I didn't know if you were frustrated because you wanted more, like I did, or because you thought last week was a mistake."

A beat, a frown. When her face finally lifted towards me all on its own, I let my fingers drop from her skin. She'd been on edge since the second I'd seen her Monday morning, and I'd waited for her to say something. To ask for more. Tell me she wasn't done. Because I most definitely wasn't, either.

But as the days rolled on and she said nothing, the less sure I was. Amusement at her pouting turned into worry, the gnawing fear that things had changed too much between us to go back to what we'd been before.

Finally, it had clicked earlier today, and I'd made the call to G before I could convince myself my hope was just the deluded pipe dream of a man who wanted this woman more than his next breath.

And now she was here, and it all made sense. It all made me want to take her over my knee.

"I'm sorry." She actually sounded sincere this time, which was an improvement. Her eyelashes fluttered as she watched me, a tender understanding washing over her expression. "I didn't think about that. I thought you were doing fine when I was a total mess because I needed..." she trailed off, that delicate flush gracing her cheekbones again.

I sighed as I lowered myself into the chair across from her. "You *needed*, Ava. And you didn't tell me. My subs are expected, *ordered*, to tell me what they need."

"I understand that. I...I couldn't get past the fact that we'd just said one night." She rubbed her forehead, a rueful smile playing across her mouth.

"*You* said just one night," I reminded her, flipping through the papers to reveal our contract from last week. "In all the years we've worked together, you've never known me to amend a contract?"

My pen slashed through the line I'd written: *"Just one night."* I initialed the change before reaching into my suit pocket to offer her favorite Mont Blanc. The one with hot pink ink that she kept in her desk drawer. Our fingers brushed when she took it from me, the simple touch electrifying the air between us.

"If I were anyone else, any other Dom, and you wanted to change the agreement or expand the contract, what would you have done?"

Her pen paused in the air, eyes snapping to mine as if magnetized. Her mouth opened to reply. Closed.

"That's what I thought. Our rules change. Boundaries, likes and dislikes." I tapped the list between us. "I expect them to. But I will not play with you if you don't tell me what you need. Understood?"

I freaking hoped the answer was yes, because I *needed* this. It had been building ever since she'd slid off my lap last week. The compulsion to get my hands on her again. Take what she gave me. Give her what she needed in return.

"Yes, I...I really am sorry. I should have said something." Pink ink scribbled underneath dark blue.

"Next time, do." I flipped the rest of the papers over, offering her the new contract.

"Of course, I...this...this is typed and printed. You had this prepared before tonight," she accused, but wonder shone in her wide eyes.

"I didn't know for sure why you were acting like an unholy terror, but I hoped." Hoped, prayed, jerked off more times this week than I probably had since college. Even though the first rule of the contract was no sex of any kind, maybe this would be enough.

I wanted to fuck her, but I couldn't see a way to do that without it impacting our working relationship. Especially after this week. Maybe that would change too, but for now, we needed that line. *I* needed it, before I barreled right over it and locked her in my basement.

She'd love it. I would, too.

"The final page is the scene I have in mind for tonight. You haven't just been difficult this week. I was also disappointed to learn you've been prioritizing work over your physical and mental well-being. I'll expect you to take your punishment accordingly."

She murmured in agreement, flushing deeper. I stilled her hand before she signed off on tonight's scene.

"You've barely read that."

"I want it." Green eyes flashed. She looked needy, greedy almost, and I tamped down on the hunger that flooded my body.

I needed to make one last point before we really got started. "Find at least one thing to modify. I won't make you every time," I allowed when her brow furrowed. "But I need to know I can trust you to tell me what you want. Consider it a test."

That furrow turned into concentration. Ava had always excelled in testing environments. After a moment, she scribbled a line at the bottom of my list. A laugh bolted out of my chest when I saw what she'd written.

"You're mandating a martini afterwards?"

"I liked that last week. It felt like I earned it." She shrugged, leaning back in her chair as I signed the page.

"You did earn it. You'll earn this one, too. Now, come."

I gathered the papers, rolling them in my hand as I entered the hallway. Last week's rules applied. As soon as she stepped out of the meeting room, the scene was on, and she was mine.

Her foot crossed the threshold.

And she was mine.

***

Some people—outsiders, mostly—might consider setup the boring part of BDSM. Stocking supplies, mentally reviewing my scene, checking gear. But for me, it was meditative. I'd had good scenes, even great ones, with little preparation, but often it took some work to get a sub to go truly euphoric, and that was my goal, generally. With Ava, always.

Plus, it had the added bonus of forcing Ava to wait in the hallway while I adjusted the private room to my liking, calling down to the front desk for what I needed. For the second time tonight, I didn't offer her a cushion. By the time I led her to stand on the thin rubber mat in the center of the room, her knees were red.

Punishment's a bitch. Then again, it's supposed to be.

I circled her as she stood, eyes on the ground, waiting.

"You've been neglecting yourself, Ava. You said you miss yoga? Let's see a sun salutation. Go."

She moved at my barked command, confusion only registering for a moment. Our contract tonight had simply stated I'd put her through a physically demanding punishment, not the exact details.

She'd been a regular practitioner since she'd had her panic attack a few years ago, and her dedication showed, her body flowing smoothly through the series of poses I'd looked up on my phone this evening on the way to the club. Down dog, standing pose, down into a plank, lower halfway, back to down dog.

"Again." Her form, from what I knew of yoga, was beautiful. She finished another round as I turned on the low music I'd queued on my phone. It trickled through the Bluetooth speaker in the corner. "Again."

On her sixth, I stopped her, taking a moment to stroke up the back of her thigh in a down dog. "This is nice. Did you wear it for me?" I tugged on the hem of her silky camisole and shorts set. Black today.

"Yes, Sir." She sounded mildly strained, not out of breath yet. Good.

"It's lovely. I can't touch under your clothes, but when you're like this, the fabric rides up." I traced the edge of her shorts where they'd slid to show the curve of her ass. I pinched it hard, making her gasp. "Continue."

I made her flow through several more rounds, stopping her whenever I felt like it, stroking my fingers across her chest as far down as her camisole would allow as she stood. Again, later to run my fingers through her hair as she was in an up dog, supported on her arms.

"You can go faster, can't you, pretty girl?" I crooned, twisting her ponytail harder. The cadence of her breath was picking up, but still even.

"Yes, Sir."

"Let's see it, then."

Either consciously or not, she matched her progression through the poses to the music. This time, I didn't stop her, watching her body, her habitual movement, take over while her mind started drifting away. It's a subtle, beautiful thing, watching a sub's eyes get softer. Muscles more pliant. Breath deepening.

"Stop," I ordered just as she was about to shoot forward from her down dog. She jerked, hovering on her toes, legs straining. My hands found the curve of her ass again, those barely-there shorts nearly revealing everything to me. Her pussy was so close to my fingers, a flicker of movement might have allowed me to touch her.

My hand smacked the inside of her leg, as high as I could without going up her shorts. The hit itself was soft, just a warmup, but she wasn't expecting it. She rose higher on her toes.

"If you work for me, you take care of yourself. That was our deal, wasn't it?" Another smack on the other side, just the slightest burn to get the blood flowing to the surface. She was ready for it this time, braced.

"Yes, Sir."

"Are you neglecting your part of our bargain?" Another smack, slightly lower. Slightly harder. Muscles twitched under black silk.

"I'm sorry, Sir."

I hit the outside of her thigh, the hardest yet. Just enough to feel the sting. I saw the moment her arms quivered slightly. "That wasn't an answer to my question. Again."

She flowed through the poses, a short reprieve for her arms. I halted her again after a few more rounds. Two smacks, a little harder. Three, a slap.

"Are you neglecting your part of our bargain?"

"Yes, Sir. I'm sorry, Sir." She flinched when I spanked her again—the hardest yet—but sank into my caress, leaning into me for the next hit. Christ, she was perfect, and she was loosening up the more I put her through her paces.

Ava was always known for being an absolute powerhouse, but her panic attack had brought all that to a screeching halt. When she'd huddled in the chair in my office, biting her lip and handing over a laughably overqualified resume, I'd known she'd needed me. I just hadn't known how.

Rebuilding Ava's confidence had been one of the easiest tasks in my job. All I had to do was give her a project, then watch her take it over one step at a time. But I'd gotten sloppy. I hadn't been watching her closely enough, and no matter how many Cheryls I threw at her, I realized now she'd always bite off more than she could chew.

Always trying to be better. More perfect. To prove she was stronger than the panic attacks she'd thought had ended her career.

Now that I knew her proclivities in kink, it was like a missing piece finally settled into place. Ava liked rules. Boundaries. Do this, reward. Do that, punishment. I realized now she'd spent the last three years on a knife's edge, waiting for some imaginary ball to drop and take her out again because she didn't know the consequences, what the lines were.

But I knew what she needed now, and I was very good at consequences. By the time her arms started shaking, her ass and thighs were
the most gorgeous red I'd ever seen, and my palm was stinging with
delicious heat. But her whole body was relaxed, dropping into deeper
and deeper poses, her eyes closing at intervals. The more she moved,
the calmer she looked, breath even as it became more shallow with her
exertion.

We floated together in that little room, my cock hard as I watched
her body move and her mind float. My palm struck against her skin at
my favorite little spot, nearly touching her cunt.

"When you don't take care of yourself, your work, your body, and
your mental health suffer. Is that the kind of assistant I deserve?" I
demanded, sounding harsh, and followed it up with five hard smacks
on her ass. She pushed up higher in the air, seeking more. I gave it to
her, watching as the fabric of her shorts moved to the side to give me
a better look at her pussy. Was it my imagination, or was a sheen of
wetness coating the peek of flesh I saw? I bit back a groan, palming my
heavy erection and squeezing through the fabric of my pants.

She was at an ideal height like this. I smacked her again, and again,
picturing it. The slip of fabric between her legs wouldn't stand a
chance when I ripped it aside. Took out my aching cock and drove it
into her without any preparation. Damn, she'd be hot and ready. If
spanking turned her on as much as her list said it did, she'd beg me for
it if she had any clue what I was thinking.

But I wouldn't tell her. Not now. Some subs would say yes to anything if they were in the right state of mind, and she was nearly there,
her body flowing with mindless, languid movements. I wouldn't take
advantage of her like this.

"I asked you a question," I spanked her again, my measured strokes
cracking over the soft strains of the music. "I expect prompt and hon-

est responses when I ask you a question. Is that the kind of assistant I deserve?"

She moaned, stretching her body to meet my hand. She loved it. "No, Sir." She was gasping, losing her grip on all that nice deep breathing she'd been doing just a few minutes ago.

"Move." She rolled like a wave, stretched up towards the ceiling, then back down. "Stop."

Her breath lurched out of her as she jerked to a halt in a push-up position. Arms bent and already trembling. I took my time, making her hold it. She could, this gorgeous, perfect girl. She'd do it for me.

"When I give you work to do, it's because I know you can handle it." I watched closely. She shook, but she could go for a bit longer. "But when you take on bullshit below your pay grade just to *soothe your own fucking ego,*" I smacked the fleshy part of her ass. She jerked, then held steady, "you can't focus where I need you. Can you?"

"No, Sir," she gasped, shaking now. I knelt down on one knee to get closer.

"When you neglect yourself, you're neglecting my favorite and most valuable asset. Were you aware of that?"

She gasped, grunted, dipped just a few centimeters before righting herself. "No, Sir."

"If you don't take care of yourself, I will do it for you." I enunciated each word, growling them into her ear like I could physically implant the concept in her brain. "First thing Monday, I want a list, a complete list, Ava, of all the shit you're working on. Every single project you're overseeing. I plan to cut you out of most of them, understand?"

"Yes...Sir." She'd give out soon, but I needed to leave her with a final lesson before she did.

"And it will not be a failure. The only failure was you deciding you needed to prove yourself by taking on extraneous shit I don't care about. Do you understand?"

"Yes, Sir."

"You are not a failure. Say it."

"I'm not...a failure." She grunted, arms shaking. So close to giving out.

"Again. Just a little longer for me, precious. You can hold it for me."

"I'm not a failure."

"Again."

"I'm not a failure."

"Again. Louder!"

"I'm not a failure," she gasped, muscles quivering. She was tapped.

"Next pose." Her arms gave out on the last syllable, and she collapsed onto the mat, panting. I gave her another few breaths to rise into an up-dog. When her head lifted, I grasped her chin. "Look at me."

Her eyes were hazy, lips curved into a dazed smile even as she panted, cheeks flushed, legs hot and red where I'd hit her. "Thank you, Master," she sighed, eyelids blinking closed, that same, sated expression she'd had last week. But better. Deeper.

My pulse matched hers—throbbing and pounding. The feel of it between my legs was nearly painful, I was so hard. I swept her up in my arms, and she went limp and boneless against me, every last shred of worry and restraint evaporating into thin air.

I settled her on the daybed up against the wall, the soft sheets rustling as she stretched out. Her hair felt thick and soft as I wrapped my fingers in it, pulling it away from her shoulders, stroking and petting every inch of skin I could reach, trailing only the lightest touches over the tender skin of her thighs.

"Perfect," I pressed kisses over her half-lidded eyes, adjusting her to tend to her legs. The lightly scented oil I rubbed on her skin would help with the pain tomorrow. I took as many liberties as I dared, inching fingers as close to the edges of her clothing as I could. She sighed and whimpered and mewled while I worked, arching and pressing closer. I methodically smoothed my palms across her skin, rubbing and stroking until she'd nearly melted into the bed.

"Tired, pretty girl?" I asked as she yawned. My fingertips swirled the oil across her temples, the light lavender scent surrounding us, lulling my movements into calm caresses. My dick still raged and strained, but it was enough to be here with her, stroking and murmuring. Enjoying the peace she felt, feeling it sink into me, too.

"Yes, Master."

"Better come here, then, before you fall asleep." I crawled in beside her, pulling her onto my chest.

She hummed with a smile. "Oh, the cuddles, this is a good part," she muttered, nuzzling her forehead into the spot in the crook of my neck she'd found last week.

"You don't think the vicious spanking was the good part? Lift up," I coaxed, feeding her a sip out of the stemless martini glass I'd kept in the mini fridge during our scene. She groaned, going even more limp, if that were possible.

"It's all the good part. I feel bad th-though," she yawned again before settling back down into her spot, apparently done with the drink. I took a sip instead. I'd have to remember to offer it up before her drowsiness sank in next time. She'd gone lax last week, too.

"Why, gorgeous?" I kissed her head, pulling the sheet over her. I'd never understand why she was so hard on herself, why she pushed to be more and better when she was so easy to be with, to adore, without changing a single thing. My fingers ghosted through her hair.

"You didn't get to have any fun."

I barked out a laugh that moved my chest, jostling her. She gripped my shirt with greedy kitten claws. My lips pressed against her head, close to her ear. "Ava, it's just like you said. *It's all the good part.*"

Chapter 9
Ava

I'd woken up on Saturday morning to a scanned copy of our D/s contract in my personal email, with a terse note to inform him if and when I wanted to make any changes. We'd plan to play on Friday nights, and other days if we were free and amenable, but our alternative relationship wouldn't touch our working one.

No kink inside the office, or during what Liam had termed "normal working hours (*actual normal people hours, Ava. Not ours.*)." Honestly, a brilliant addition because Liam and I tended to work the way most people breathed.

Secure in the knowledge that we'd have Fridays to act on this new simmering awareness between us, life went back to...normal. Ish.

Being around him felt different now that I didn't have to hide any hint of my interest. Our gazes lingered longer than they used to, smiles a little more knowing than before. His voice, his scent, the brush of his sleeve against my skin as he held a door open for me, all hit different now that I knew just how masterfully he could command my body and mind.

But life moved on despite the new underlying attraction that zipped beneath every exchange we had.

On Monday, true to his word, he'd taken one look at the project list I'd painstakingly drafted and unceremoniously slashed it in half, sending items to Cheryl or other Wildes staffers. Under normal circumstances, it would have devastated me, but Liam's words kept ringing in my ears. I wasn't a failure. It wasn't that I *couldn't* handle everything, but that I didn't need to.

With my mental space freed up from fixating on him and about ten thousand random tasks, I could actually concentrate on the stuff I needed to. Like how VestedAI was suddenly a massive pain in my ass.

"The files they're sending over are fine, but I keep running into issues with the numbers," I griped, tugging on Winston's leash as we walked out of the building.

"You think they're feeding you bad data?"

Liam's hands rested casually in his pockets, jacket draped over his wrist. He looked so Wall Street cool, his aviators tilting in my direction as his collar brushed across the cursive ink on his neck. My heart fluttered, and I remembered how his hand felt against my skin. The slap of his palm on my ass. Wondered what he'd feel like in other places.

"No," I shoved the thought away. *Focus, Ava.* "The data mostly checks out. It's just always some adjustment they need to make or a file issue or something. It's small, but frustrating. They're a young company. We might need to be more hands-on with them than we want."

Liam winced, reaching for Winston's leash when he nearly jerked my arm out of my socket. My pup immediately heeled, and I huffed in annoyance. Winston had always been a pushover for Liam. Maybe he got that from me. "I don't know. I'm still not sure Masters is the partner we want," he mused out loud, wrapping the leash around his wrist.

I stopped dead in my tracks. "You shitting me right now? He's the hottest ticket in town, and he *will be ours*." I clicked my fingers in

Liam's face while I spoke, hoping to snap him out of whatever freaking stroke he was having.

"I know, but I'm just saying, I'm not sure I like the guy. And now their numbers are frustrating you? The numbers queen? Something doesn't smell right."

"That's the massive dump Winnie took in the flower beds over there. Ben says the guy was fine after you got off to a rocky start. The numbers...it's fine. I just need to dig in more."

"If you say it's nothing to worry about..."

"It's nothing to worry about." I'd make sure of it. This was my biggest priority, and I had buckets of time free now. Vested would be ours.

Liam stood close, head tipped down to scan my face. I wasn't sure what he was looking for, but the fluttering sensation that had tickled my belly all week cranked up.

I'd always been good at reading him; we worked like a well-oiled machine. One brain, two bodies. I had files on his desk before he asked for them. Meetings set up before he thought of it.

And now, I knew when he was thinking about sex. Or, more specifically, I knew when he was thinking about our time together at Dragon. It hadn't taken long for me to decipher that hot, new expression he got when he looked at me sometimes. The one that felt stripped down and secret. Illicit.

The look he was giving me right now. And just like every time I'd seen it this week, I wanted to give in to the nagging at the back of my mind. To ask, *is this enough for you? Do you want more?*

Because I want more.

"Ava," he started, inching closer.

"Yeah?" It was Wednesday. Did he want an extra night this week? Tonight? I had a hot date with my spreadsheets, but I'd drop my numbers in a heartbeat if Liam gave me a chance to crawl back into his lap. The corner of his mouth quirked like he could hear my thoughts.

"Ms. Anderson! Mr. Wildes!"

We turned to watch the man jog toward us. He was my age, mid-thirties at the most, and was wearing a typical tech company t-shirt and jeans. His sneakers had a hole in the toe.

"Can I help you?" Liam shifted to stand between me and the man speeding toward us, Winston padding with him. He screeched to a halt, light brown hair flopping over his brow as my two favorite males on the planet stared him down. "I'm Cameron Hawks. I've been trying to get in touch with you."

I frowned. "You're the one who keeps leaving messages with Cheryl?"

"Yes. And it's imperative you hear what I have to say."

"Ava, who is this?" Liam looked about two seconds away from beckoning the security guard from inside the building. I rubbed my forehead, trying to remember what I knew about Cameron Hawks, who I'd promptly expelled from my brain after reading his first message to me weeks ago.

"Masters's ex-partner. Co-founded VestedAI."

Liam glared. "Vested hasn't disclosed any other founders."

"I left the company, alright? A year ago." Cameron put his hands up like he was pleading. "I know you're making a bid—a lot of people are—but please hear me out. No one else will give me the time of day, but you need to look deeper. He's only got vaporware."

Liam looked to me for confirmation, but I shook my head. "We're doing our due diligence. Our team has plenty of experience with the product."

"No, he has a framework to make it seem legit, but I'm telling you, the algorithm isn't there. You take over, get into bed with Masters, and it'll be the biggest mistake of your life."

"Our company, including Ms. Anderson, is perfectly capable of vetting our partners. If you'll excuse us." Liam's hand on my back guided me away to the town car waiting on the street. "Let me drive you home," he muttered.

"Yeah," I agreed, craning my neck to see Cameron standing on the sidewalk, staring after us, looking dejected, hands clenching at his sides.

"What was that about?" Liam asked when the car rolled away from the curb. I shrugged, watching Winston settle in the floorboards, cramming his massive body into the tiny space. His favorite way to ride in a car, the weirdo.

"When I started getting his messages, I assumed it was a Winklevoss situation. Someone who had stakes in the beginning, jealous that he cut out too soon."

"Yeah, that seems right."

"Still though..." I mused, eyes scanning the buildings and pedestrians as they streamed outside the window. "Maybe worth a second glance. Just in case."

"You want me to take a look?"

A week ago, his question would have sent me into a tailspin, worried he thought I couldn't handle this on my own.

You are not a failure. I thought about all the work he'd taken off my plate, almost solely so I could focus on this. And I had more time to give to this project now, I really did.

"No, I'm good." I could feel his eyes on me and waited a few seconds before I glanced back at him. "Honestly, I'll check around about Hawks, and I really think the numbers are just minimal errors. I know this is a make-or-break deal for us. I'm on it."

"If you feel like you need some extra support, let me know."

I gave him a half-smile. He wasn't sneaky when he went around using words like "support" when he really meant "help."

"Will do."

***

"Still?" Winston cocked his head at Whitney's shrill tone. She was half-dressed in her black work bustier and painted-on leather pants, lips red and eyes glaring. "Not even at work?" She demanded, stomping her heeled foot on my living room floor.

"No work play. It's one of the rules." I smiled indulgently at my neighbor as she shoved her hands onto her hips.

"Why did you agree to that rule? That's a stupid rule."

"How do you know I'm not the one who requested it?" I challenged, finally closing my laptop for the night. I wouldn't get any peace until Whitney had headed out to Dragon, and VestedAI's numbers were making my brain feel wobbly, anyway.

Maybe I needed to call it a night, have some wine and watch something before bed.

"I'm about to open a red, you want some?"

"Not tonight," Whitney pointed a finger at me. "And don't play innocent. I know you didn't put that rule in your contract. You want Liam Wildes so badly your tongue practically falls out of your mouth when you talk about him."

I glared from behind the bottle opener. "Not true."

"Yes, true. And he looks at you like you're a steak."

A snort rocketed out of my body the same moment the cork popped. "The last time you saw us together, it was at a sex club. Everyone looks at each other like steak at Dragon."

Whitney draped herself across one of my barstools. "Trust me, this is different. You want him, and he wants you. Come on, you're not an idiot. You *know* he wants you. So why. Haven't. You. Hit. That. Yet." She tapped a pristinely manicured, fire-red fingernail on the quartz to punctuate her words. I splashed a little extra into my glass.

Because she was right. I *wasn't* stupid, and I saw the way he looked at me now. Those side-eye glances in between meetings, or when I caught him zoning out, staring at me like...well, like I was a steak.

The more I thought about it, the more I could convince myself that he'd maybe even been giving me these looks the whole time we'd worked together. Maybe he had felt the same attraction I had since day one, and now we were finally able to express it within the boundaries of the club.

"It's complicated," I finally answered, succumbing to her piercing stare before taking a huge swig of wine, as if that could save me from this conversation.

"You're both absolute smokeshows and have the same kinks. I see the issue." She nodded sagely, arching her eyebrows like I was full of it.

"He's my boss. We work together. It's messy when it's outside the club."

Whitney's arch look turned thoughtful. "Is it? I thought you said this week was better since you had some boundaries in place."

"It was. It *is*, I mean, I'm not totally freaking out anymore, but I still think about him all the time. And this weekend was so good, Whit, you have no clue. And he hasn't even *done* anything to me yet."

My voice lowered because I could only talk about The Spanking with hushed reverence.

"Alright, so you're thinking about fucking him, and you can't, because of the rules. Other than that, everything is okay? Nothing weird has happened? He hasn't tried to spit in your mouth in front of a client or something?"

"He's a professional, and so am I. That would never happen."

More sage nodding. "Got it. So, you're right. It is complicated, I need to amend my statement."

"Thank you for understandi—"

"You're absolute smokeshows and have the same kinks, you're really good at sticking to the boundaries you put up, and the only thing causing any issues is your agreement not to have sex. Right?"

I replayed her words. "Uh."

"Because if he's feeling this tension even a little bit, I bet he'd agree that you could still keep things professional even if he was railing you nightly. In fact," Whitney talked over me when I tried to stutter something coherent to counter her. Her finger sliced through the air. "I bet focusing at work would actually be *easier*, because you wouldn't have all this pent-up sexual tension."

I swirled my wine around as I thought about what she was saying. It was so appealing. There was a gratuitous, hedonistic sort of logic to it. Thinking about him all the time was distracting, to say the least, even though we were good about pushing that aside during working hours. So, wouldn't it make sense to remove the distraction? Take our partnership to the next level, physically?

God, I'd love that. I could still feel his fingers in my hair, his palm on my ass. The way he watched me, controlled me, would be perfect when both of us were naked. Like life-alteringly, mind-numbingly perfect, I just knew it. But it still seemed like too much of a risk.

"Players have very fulfilling kink lives that don't include sex, Whitney," I lectured, as if she didn't spend more time at the club than I did.

"I know, hun. But can you?"

She left in a waft of perfume that smelled simultaneously like cake and sex, leaving me staring out the floor-to-ceiling windows at the city beyond, glass half empty already.

While I ate my meal-prepped dinner, I FaceTimed my parents, because nothing squashes sexual ponderings like seeing the inside of your childhood kitchen. By the time I crawled into bed to watch some TV and pass out, I was on the very edge of convincing myself that Whitney didn't know what she was talking about. The absolute cusp. I was practically already convinced.

Liam's name flashed across my phone, and my heart thumped so hard I worried he could hear it in my voice.

"Hey. Did you see the updated presentation I sent for Baker tomorrow?" I answered before he could speak. My fingers clenched in my duvet because I was being ridiculous. It wasn't out of the ordinary for him to call me this late. "The intro slides look better."

I waited through three painfully long seconds before he cleared his throat on the other end. "I didn't call to talk about work."

Seven words were my downfall, my absolute undoing. Seven words were all it took for me to realize the gut-wrenching truth. Whitney was right. I needed more from him. I needed sex, and late-night calls, and to know what he felt like against my body. And even though I shifted at the persistent ache between my thighs that suddenly felt like a living thing, I told myself to calm down. He probably didn't mean...that.

"Oh. Can't sleep? I hear a glass of warm milk does wonders." That was me. Cool and quippy, unflappable in the face of my smoking hot boss calling me after nine p.m. on a Wednesday.

His low laugh scratched across the line, and I crossed one thigh over the other. "I'll keep that in mind. I'm calling about last Friday, actually." A familiar squeak in the background told me he was in the chair in his home office. I could picture him, leaning back, one leg crossed over the other, staring at his ceiling with a glass of scotch in his hand.

I gulped. "Okay."

"I usually follow up with subs several days after a session. How are you doing? Physically? Emotionally?"

Ah. Well, that was very nice of him, and honestly something I should have seen coming. These kinds of follow-ups were best practice in our world. A lot of things could go down in a scene that someone might not fully process in the moment. If I had a problem with something, discussing it after the fact was best for everyone.

"I'm great, physically and emotionally."

"Glad to hear it. Was there anything in particular you liked that I should keep in mind? Didn't like?"

My breath matched my heartbeat, galloping even though I tried to will myself into a semblance of calm.

"You'll recall, Ava, that I require complete honesty from my subs." Damn. That voice snapped me to attention like a shot of adrenaline. I couldn't disobey him. I didn't want to.

"I loved everything about it, Sir."

In the silence between us, his breath grounded mine, slow and steady. I worked to match, every fiber of my being beating against my skin, screaming at me to tell him I wanted more. Tell him I loved every minute except I hadn't wanted him to stop at spanking. That I wanted him to fuck me until I couldn't walk.

"Everything?"

"All of it," I breathed, because I wasn't sure if now was the time to ask for that. Over the phone? Late at night?

"Calling you was a bad idea."

"Oh, yeah?" I winced. Subs were eager by nature. Surely, I hadn't put him off or made him uncomfortable by being so effusive about loving last Friday. Maybe he would have preferred me to give him some actual constructive criticism.

"I'm going to be hard enough to pound nails for the rest of the night."

A relieved laugh bubbled out of me, my shoulders slumping. "Sorry?"

"Don't apologize." I could hear him move in his chair, adjusting? Taking his cock out? The image of him stroking himself while he talked to me went to my head faster than the wine from earlier. "I should be used to it by now. The memory of your skin so pink and pretty...it's been driving me to distraction all week."

Yes. *Yes.* This was what I needed. Confirmation he was feeling this, too. He was having just as hard a time as I was compartmentalizing everything. I bit my lip, rolling to my back. Maybe I *should* say something...ask...

"You took it so well, Ava. It plays in my mind constantly."

Oh, what an opening. I grinned up at my ceiling. "What do you do when you think about it?"

"Ava." A growl, a warning I couldn't find it in myself to heed. Right here, in bed, in the dark, he wasn't my boss, but he wasn't my Dom either. Instead, it felt like some heady mixture of the two that I wanted to explore more than I wanted to breathe.

"We should do something about it if it's been bothering you all week. I could walk you through it. I can lead very productive calls, as you know."

His muffled, breathy curse felt like a physical touch on my skin. "You're going to kill me."

"Touch yourself, Liam. You know you want to." The game I was playing was dangerous, but it didn't feel like it. It felt hot and tingly and like if I pushed harder, just went one level deeper with him, it would open the doors to all that *more* I wanted from him.

"Of course I want to," he groaned and I could already picture it, his zipper sliding down, his palm covering his dick. "Know what else I want, precious?"

"Tell me."

"For you to stop teasing me and go the fuck to sleep."

"Liam." My turn to groan, or, really, it came out as a whine.

"I'm glad you enjoyed last week. Your feedback is noted, but we have that Baker presentation tomorrow, and I need you sharp."

"But—"

"Now hang up, close your eyes, and go to sleep thinking about me jacking myself raw while I picture the way your ass jiggles when I spank you."

"Liam, I—"

"'Yes, Sir' would be the answer I'm looking for."

God, that voice was back, and as much as I hated him telling me to hang up, to give up the game I'd tried to push him into, I loved the way it made my nerve endings come alive.

"Yes, Sir."

"And Ava, under no circumstances are you allowed to come until next Friday. No toys, not with your fingers, nothing. Understood?"

My eyes slid to the side table where my favorite vibrator was already waiting for me, just like it had been all week, because once I'd gotten a single taste of Liam, I suddenly couldn't get enough.

"Ava." Warning, sharp and controlled, threaded through his voice. I bit my lip. I wanted him *here*. I wanted to play. I wanted an orgasm, dammit.

"Yes, Sir."

Silence pulled taut between us before the line went dead. I chucked my phone to the end of the bed.

Chapter 10
Ava

"Come on," I gritted, urging the little metal teeth to slide through the zipper casing. But just as it had been for the last five minutes, it was stuck. Stuck like someone had superglued the damn thing.

Downstairs, I heard the clang of cutlery, and the voices of the caterers and florists transforming Liam's main floor for our investor party. I still had some time before people started showing up, but the clock was ticking, and I wanted to get down there to make sure everything was going smoothly.

"Damn. Shit. Dammit," I cursed, twisting again to get to the back of my dress and banging my elbow, again.

Knock knock.

I froze on the wall of Liam's guest bathroom. I'd been pressed up against it to get some sort of leverage as I wrestled the fabric into submission, and when I thought about it, Liam's bathroom *was* on the other side. *Shit.*

"You good, Anderson? Sounds like you're getting mugged in there." His voice was muffled, but still clear enough that I could hear his laughter, low and rolling. Ugh, it made my stomach clench.

"Just..." I leaned forward, bracing against the blue-tiled counter. My head hung as I finally accepted my fate. "Need help with my zipper."

He didn't respond, but he didn't need to. In seconds, soft, creaking strides made their way down the hallway. I braced entirely differently, but still wasn't prepared when he stepped through his guest room into the attached bathroom.

His white shirt was completely unbuttoned, collar gaping to reveal almost all the intertwining tattoos I usually only got glimpses of throughout the day. *Ad Astra Per Aspera.* The words swirled across the base of his neck, looping calligraphy arching around Dali's melting clocks and a Fibonacci spiral that flowed over his pec. Something floral I'd never gotten a good look at wrapped around his ribs, disappearing behind the open fabric.

My eyes took a hard left to trace the etched lines of his abs, all the way to where his pants were unbuttoned and only partially zipped, like he hadn't bothered to finish fastening them before coming straight to me.

"You look defeated," he murmured, standing close enough behind me that I could feel his body heat, warm and tempting. His eyes skimmed my dress, black, low-backed and high-necked with long sleeves. Just short enough to be flirty.

"I am defeated." I hung my head, partially to make him laugh, and partially because I didn't need to keep staring at his devastatingly handsome face. That body I couldn't have.

Aside from normal business stuff, he hadn't said a word to me after hanging up a couple of days ago. He hadn't even said anything about tonight. Friday. The night that was supposed to be *ours*.

I had assumed we wouldn't be getting up to anything. Our focus needed to be firmly on the partners and the next round investors we were hoping to woo. But even though I understood our priorities, I couldn't help but feel a flutter of disappointment that he hadn't even acknowledged it.

His hands were warm, one firm on my waist while the other grasped the zipper. I shivered when the knuckle of his index finger brushed against my spine.

This had probably been a bad idea. I should have gone downstairs and asked Wesley or one of the caterers for help. Instead, I stood alone, nearly pressed against the man of my wildest fantasies, wishing with everything I had that he'd pull the zipper down instead of up.

"You're tense. Everything alright?"

"Fine." I cleared my throat and tried again. "Just an important night."

The zipper gave slightly, rising an inch. "You sure?"

"Of course."

Was it my imagination, or did his hand flex against my hip, pulling me a millimeter closer? "Ava." His breath stirred the strands of hair I'd artfully pulled out of my French twist, fluttering across my neck. Goosebumps followed in their wake.

His voice was low, and so was mine when I whispered back. "Yeah?"

"I know when you're lying, pretty girl." The zipper gave way, gliding all the way up as Liam pressed a soft, barely-there kiss under my ear. I was trembling now, desire and anticipation flooding my body with heat.

"Did you touch yourself this week?" He kept his hands on me, petting my waist, fingers holding my hip even tighter, closer. My eyes fluttered closed, surrendering to the possessive control of his grip, like he could move me however he wanted and he knew I'd stay there.

"No, Sir. Not after you told me not to." Another kiss, this time accompanied by the scrape of teeth across my skin. I moaned, tilting my head to the side to give him more access. He didn't take the invitation, instead ducking down to whisper in my ear.

"Such a goddamn good girl, Ava. Exactly what I wanted."

I was melting, absolutely collapsing under his praise. He sounded so pleased, so sincere and filthy. He would have no way of knowing if I'd had my way with every vibrator in my collection. But he believed me, he trusted me, and that in and of itself was a reward I hadn't known I needed.

I sighed, relaxing into him. I *did* need this, because I was telling the truth. No matter what it felt like to have his attention on me almost all day every day, or how it felt to remember his voice and his hands and his *words* from this weekend...I hadn't touched myself in days.

"It *is* Friday, you know. Do you want to play?"

"Yes." *God, yes.* "Please," I added for good measure, because he liked when I asked for what I wanted.

My attention was still focused on the line where the mirror met the tile of the vanity, but from the corner of my eye, I saw his mouth curl up in a smirk. "We don't have to. We have about thirty minutes before Ben gets here, and I'm sure there are things you need to see to."

Was he right? Of course, but when he rolled his hips against my lower back, it wasn't really a choice. He was hard as steel. Had he been as hungry for this as I was? Would he let me feel him? Bring him pleasure? I wanted to so badly, but we had boundaries in place, lines I worried he wouldn't cross, ever.

"Please, Master. I want you to play with me." *However you want, anything you want*, I silently begged.

His hand glided up the front of my body, smoothing over my breasts before his fingers curled around my throat, the heat, the control, searing through skin and muscle to imprint him into my bones.

"Look at me." His fingertips pressed into delicate skin as he growled in my ear. A sweet heat speared between my legs. Our eyes met in the mirror as my head raised, he looked dark and satisfied, like a hunter who knew he'd already cornered his prey. And I looked flushed and excited, like I wanted him to catch me.

"Lift your skirt up."

The black fabric slid up my thighs at his command. Where the hem lifted, his hand followed, swooping down to caress every inch of newly-exposed skin.

"The problem with our touching rule, is I can only feel the skin I can see. And sometimes you wear so many damn clothes, it's all I can do to find an inch." His fingers stroked, then pinched the skin on the inside of my leg, so close to my pussy I felt the muscles clench. I watched him watching me in the mirror, his eyes darting around the exposed skin as my skirt finally cleared my ass.

Even though he hadn't said anything about playing tonight, I'd picked the black lacy underwear for him. His hand tightened on my throat as he groaned.

"Are you ready for it, precious? Have you been thinking about this as much as I have?"

"Probably more, Sir."

"Not possible. Pull your panties down. That's far enough," he stopped me when the underwear reached the top of my knees. My heart was pounding, but I didn't think about how this was the first time he'd seen me naked. I just wanted to expose as much of myself to him as I could. Shove everything at him and watch him handle it all.

His gaze zeroed in on my bare, glistening skin. "Already?"

"Yes, Sir."

His eyes narrowed, jaw flexing under freshly shaved skin that I wanted to feel along every curve of my body. "Show me."

I bit my lip as I stroked between my legs, shuddering at the feeling of my fingers right there, when I'd been craving this for days. They came away wet. Liam grabbed my wrist in a nearly punishing grip, yanking my hand, twisting my arm awkwardly to take my fingers in his mouth.

He moaned, pressing his hips against me again, flexing hard enough to bump me into the counter. A groan stuttered out of my mouth. The move felt too much like a thrust, moving me, grinding my mound against the edge of the cool tiles of the vanity. Goosebumps broke out along my skin.

"Maybe you have been thinking about this as much as I have." He dropped my hand, watching it fall to the tile. "So good," he murmured, thrusting again. His cock throbbed against the open fly of his pants, the thin fabric of his boxers the only thing between me and his straining flesh. I wanted it gone.

"Touch yourself, Ava. Make yourself come." He braced his hands on either side of mine, trapping me against the counter, allowing only a few inches of space for my hand to trail down the soft swell of my stomach before settling over my clit. My fingers moved in a circular motion I usually used to warm up, but I was already so gone, they slipped through easily.

With Liam's heat at my back and his gaze riveted on my hand, even the slightest touch felt like an imminent explosion. I shuddered as I circled the bud of my clit, fireworks ricocheting through my body. I wanted to savor it, the slow slide, the heat of his gaze. My eyes fluttered closed, the heady feeling of captivating him like this, performing for him, tightening my core.

Smack.

I gasped, eyes flying open in time to see Liam's hand return to the counter. The hand on my throat tightened. "Eyes on me, Ava. And stop playing with yourself. I told you to come. I want two fingers inside that cunt now."

My throat spasmed under his palm, struggling to gulp air as I followed his instructions. His dark eyes turned vicious and wild as he watched me, like he couldn't tear them away. His undivided attention, his own heaving breaths at my back, pushed me closer to the edge. I was hot, heavy with need from the last few days, and this was almost everything I wanted. Almost.

"You need something filling you up, pretty girl. I know it. Add another finger. Stroke yourself. Yes, perfect."

My head lolled onto his shoulder, leaning more of my weight on him as the new feelings surged through me and splintered. I was heading for my climax quickly, more quickly than I'd ever come before. But his words, his body, his attention—it was everything.

"Tell me how you feel, precious. What would I feel if I was fucking you?"

I groaned, eyes nearly fluttering closed. His intensifying grip on my neck didn't help things. I wanted him to steal my oxygen, black me out on him. Go under with all this hot pleasure swirling around me. I wet my lips, working hard to keep my mind focused enough to answer him. I was so close, so, so...

"Hot. Slick."

"More, Ava. What am I missing?"

How could I describe it to him? The desperate clutching of my body around my hand, the soul-deep desire to have *him* there, and not just me. "I want you. It should be you."

It wasn't an answer to his question, but it didn't matter. His eyes went black as the hand he'd clenched on the counter flattened across my own pumping fingers.

"I know you do, sweetheart. I'd fuck you so good. Hit that spot you need. Make you scream." His palm pressed against the back of my hand, putting more pressure at the apex of my thighs, rocking harder and faster than I had been.

I matched him without a thought, crying out when his thumb brushed against my lips, so close to where I needed him. "You'd love it. How I'd stretch you. Smack your ass and turn you over and make you take it again and again and again."

The image he conjured, the pace he set, the feeling of him working my hand between my legs...it was all too much. I came with a deep moan that clawed its way out of my throat. Waves of pleasure broke over me as Liam pressed our hips into the counter, more pressure to sharpen the edge of release.

Through it all, he murmured in my ear about how perfect I was, how gorgeous I sounded, how he wanted me so badly he could barely function. Finally, as the last shuddering pulses of pleasure wrung out of me, I fell against him, drooping in his arms. He kept his hand over mine between my legs like he owned it, even though he'd never touched me there.

"Feel better?" he purred as I panted against him. My fingers were still trapped inside me, but moving my hand would have meant moving his, and in that moment I'd have rather died.

"Yes. Thank you, Sir."

"You earned it." His fingers slid from my throat to caress a stray strand of hair back from my face, so at odds with the firm pressure he still exerted on my most intimate flesh. "You needed to relax, and I need to give you what you need."

In one swift move, he whirled, shoving my back against the wall beside us. My head thumped against it as he crowded into my space, kicking my legs further apart, stretching my underwear where it still fell above my knees.

"But this next is just for me. You'll still take it, won't you?"

"Yes, Sir."

He groaned in the back of his throat, palm slanting across my neck again to pin me in place. "So eager, and you don't even know what I have planned."

I didn't *care* what he had planned. I'd take anything he gave me and probably still want more. I'd thought just playing with him would be enough, but two weeks in and it wasn't even close. How had I ever thought I could do this without touching him, feeling him inside me? I'd do anything he asked without a second thought.

"I want what you give me, Master."

His forehead pressed against mine, his grunt sounded like it was ripped out of him. Head down, I had the perfect view of how he took himself out of his boxers, stroked his cock with a casual, unhurried pace.

My mouth watered. He was long and thick. Of course he was, I'd felt him pressed up against me more than once. But seeing him was different than just feeling.

"You're such a good girl, Ava," he murmured, pressing my throat harder. "But you get up in your own head. So wound up. And we both know I can't spank you in the middle of the party later, can I?"

My mouth went dry as I watched his slow, methodical stroking.

"So, how can I remind you to relax? That your job is done, and you've performed it flawlessly, and all you have to do tonight is be the brilliant, charming, peerless woman I know?" His hand moved faster, speeding as if the thought of me was enough to turn him on. His thumb shifted from the side of my neck, brushing up my jaw to stroke against my lips. My mouth fell open on instinct, and he pushed his finger inside.

He rocked forward, closer, when I sucked on him, helpless to the desire thrumming through my veins. The tip of his cock brushed the bare skin between my legs, and I swear I felt the echo of our moans in the very core of myself, the absolute fabric of my being.

His thumb pushed deeper, and I sucked him harder, wanting more. I wanted to drop to my knees and take something else in my mouth. Hear him make that helpless groan again.

"Don't even think about it."

His thumb disappeared in an instant as he wrapped hard fingers around my jaw, like he could hear my thoughts. A whimper left me before I could catch myself, still staring at his hand as it pumped faster, furiously stroking.

"I know you want it. You don't think I want it, too? To see those lips wrapped around my dick? Lipstick staining my skin like you own me?" His fingers gripped my jaw tighter as he stroked even faster, beating himself off now. Every few seconds, his cock brushed against me in the most torturous rhythm.

"But we have rules, and I am always, always in control." Liam pressed his face closer to mine. His rough, panting breaths huffed against my skin. "So, if I can't come down your pretty throat, and I can't keep you in line—keep you focused—tonight, I'll have to get creative."

His hand floated down my body, pausing to pinch my nipple where it strained against the fabric of my dress, making me gasp. I wanted more, I wanted it *harder*, but he was already gone, fingers skimming down to hook into the sides of my panties, pulling them up.

"Watch, precious. Watch while I remind you who you fucking belong to." Cum spewed out of his cock before he was even done speaking, his final words almost lost in his groan. He splattered across my pussy, bumping again and again against the smooth skin. Too much for it to be a coincidence. He was getting off on me.

He moaned as his hand finally slowed, dripping into my underwear, soaking the silk. He dipped his head to rest against the wall next to mine, like he could barely hold it up as he pulled the fabric up my hips, taking time to brush his fingers across the smooth silk, pressing his spend against my skin.

His head lifted just enough to look me in the eye, our panting breaths and the smell of sex heavy in the air. He swayed closer, eyes darting, I swore, to my mouth. I arched forward, seeking, needing his lips on mine.

"Stay." He ordered, shoving away from the wall. Cold air rushed against my skin, shocking some semblance of sense into me. I stayed put, staring as he cleaned up at the sink, the feeling of him wet and sticky between my thighs.

His face was taut and serious as he carefully dried his hands, taking in every inch of skin like he was cataloguing it for later while he slid my skirt back down. He straightened and smoothed as if it was imperative that everything look neat and ordered to hide the absolute wreck he'd made inside my panties.

"I want—" I blurted, biting my lip to stop the words from bursting out.

He gripped my waist like he had every right to do so. I pressed further into the wall as he lifted my chin. "What do you want?"

I shouldn't have said anything. What did I even really want? No boundaries, no rules, was a dangerous place for a D/s couple to be. Especially a new one. But he didn't feel new to me. He felt safe and hot and like I could have every inch of him, and it still wouldn't be enough.

"Prompt and honest responses," he warned, leaning closer, the smallest threat.

I took a steadying breath. "I want to update the rules."

His head cocked, and a little smile flirted at the edges of his mouth, like he already knew what I was going to say. "What would you like to change?"

He sounded amused and dangerous, but I forced the words out. I'd promised him...this is what he'd told me he wanted. For me to speak up. "I want you to kiss me. Fuck me. Please, Sir."

I sounded a little breathy and desperate, but hell, I *felt* breathy and desperate. His eyes flicked to my mouth like he was thinking about doing it right that second.

"Changing the game this much this early is a slippery slope."

"I know, but..." I wasn't whining. I *wasn't whining*. I just needed him to know the effect he had on me, and I needed to know if he felt it, too.

"I know, sweetheart. It's all I can think about." His thumb pressed into my chin, turning my head this way and that, looking for a trace of a lie. "I know how to separate work and play. Things can stay the same at the office. But are you sure about this? You're not asking just because I'm dripping between your thighs right now and you want another orgasm? Greedy," he accused, mouth tipping up in a charming, wicked smile.

Mine perked up in response. I *did* want another orgasm, but it was more than that. I'd always been attracted to him, but now, knowing how he read me, how he controlled me...I needed more.

"I know what I'm asking for, Liam." I used his name on purpose, his partner, not his playmate. His eyes flashed. "If you'd like to give it."

"Pretty girl, I want to give you everything you ask for and then all the things you wouldn't even think to ask. I'll fuck you. I'll kiss this gorgeous mouth. Anything else you want?"

You. The answer was so obvious, so loud in my head, I was surprised he couldn't hear it. I wanted all of him, not just bits and pieces at the club or the office. But that seemed like too much to ask. "No, Sir."

Liam smirked, leaning forward to press his mouth next to mine. Not quite a kiss, but closer than we'd ever been before.

"Don't forget, precious," he whispered, lips taking a stinging bite at the corner of my mouth, making me shudder. "I can tell when you lie."

Chapter 11
Ava

"—can't wait to see what you have up your sleeve next." Andrea Smithson lowered her voice, like we were conspiring together. I gave her a wicked grin in return. She hadn't said a word about seeing me at Dragon, but something had changed since then. Our conversation tonight was productive enough to make me think she was leaning toward working with us.

"You know Liam's always got something going."

"I wasn't talking about Liam. Word on the street is that you're about to land this big fish nearly all by yourself." Her head tilted to the front door where Mark Masters was shucking his coat, handing it to one of the servers.

"It's a group effort, really. But on that note, if you'll excuse me."

Andrea turned to talk to someone behind her. Liam's living room was crowded enough to be practically buzzing with partners, investors, and prospects. Wesley was a little high-maintenance, but he'd done a good job taking this to the finish line.

A satisfied feeling sat warm in my chest that had nothing to do with the orgasm from earlier, or the wetness in my underwear. This was going off without a hitch. Everyone in their place, like a perfect puzzle that had clicked together after months of planning. And the last piece had just arrived.

"Mark," I called out, already reaching my hand to shake his. "Glad you could make it."

"Pleasure's all mine, Ava." Mark was dressed like every other man here—perfectly tailored suit, combed hair. His eyes glinted like the polished leather of his shoes, and I tried not to notice his survey of my body. His gaze snapped up quickly enough for me to write the glance off as nerves, perhaps, or just sizing me up.

"Don't hog the girl, Mark. I know how little of Ms. Anderson there is to go around."

That voice, the smarmy implication that I wasn't enough, it all hit me like a slap to the face. Stunning and uncivilized.

Victor Rathers, CEO at Nexus Holdings, the firm I'd sold my soul to until I'd had nothing left to give. He sauntered through the front door, already tossing his coat at the server.

My heart thudded, pissing me off. Victor didn't have any hold over me anymore, but old habits were hard to break, and I would always, always associate him with the icy heat of inadequacy. Fear.

I forced myself to smile. "Victor."

"I kid, Ava. Just a joke. Lovely, as always." He took my hand before I could offer it, his silvering head dipping to brush a kiss across the back. I held in a gag. His lips were slimy on my skin.

Mark's eyes bounced between us, eyebrows rising. "Victor mentioned you're all old friends of his. Thought it would be fun to bring him along as a plus-one."

I practically yanked my hand away, resisting the urge to wipe it on my dress. I opened my mouth to...Damn, what could I do? I couldn't alienate our biggest potential asset for the next funding round, and if Victor stayed at this party, I'd run in front of the nearest taxi.

"A plus one usually means a date." Liam's amused voice broke through my scrambling thoughts. I felt him before I saw him, a comforting, imposing presence at my elbow. "But we don't judge here."

Irritation flashed across Mark's face, but Victor chuckled lightly. "Always have something witty to say, don't you, Wildes? That legendary charm."

Neither man offered his hand, instead eyeing each other from opposing sides of the entryway.

"I'm afraid you've been misled, Masters. Victor doesn't have any friends here." Liam sounded calm, but I could see the muscle in his jaw tic.

"Oh, I can see a few." Victor craned his neck to investigate the room behind us, waving at someone in the crowd. That, more than anything, was my biggest worry.

CEO of the largest PE-firm in the city, Victor knew everyone and everything that went on in our world. There were people here who were old customers or partners of his, and I was sure he was actively scoping the room, picking out faces he could try to poach later. "Sorry I bent the truth a bit, Masters. But I couldn't miss the opportunity to be a fly on the wall. Scope out a minor competitor."

"If you still think we're minor, you're not paying attention, Victor. Must be slipping." Liam sounded breezy, teasing even, but I knew he wanted Victor out as much as I did. His barb should have hit—my old boss prided himself on having a finger on the pulse of everything happening in the private equity world. But he brushed the comment aside like it was a remark about the weather. His eyes narrowed on me instead.

"Ava, my little protégé. So glad you found your place here. Not everyone is cut out for the big time. This all seems much more your speed. Planning parties. Getting coffee for the people running the real business."

I reminded myself that if I slapped him, he'd use it against me. His words shouldn't have affected me so deeply, but he was right, of course. I hadn't been cut out to work with him. I hadn't been able to keep pace.

"Coffee, managing the staff, orchestrating due diligence, directing our portfolio..." Liam stepped closer, looming over me. "Real minor-league shit she's working on."

For the first time tonight, Victor's face twisted into a broad grin, flashing teeth like lightning in a storm. "Nice of you to throw her some bones. Be sure not to overdo it, though. Been keeping her out of the hospital?"

I heard a murmur behind me. A quick glance told me everything I needed to know. The din of the party was slowly dying down as more people turned their attention to the little drama unfolding in the foyer. Masters' head was pinging back and forth like he was watching a tennis match.

For once in my life, my voice had dried up. Just minutes ago, I had felt so close to the success I'd dreamed of at this company, in my career. And it was all crashing down around me. More reminders that I wasn't good enough. That this support role would be all I'd ever amount to. Because I couldn't handle the pressure of doing the real work.

"Yeah, I haven't had a problem with that. Amazing how far some basic human decency can go." Liam stepped forward, and I grabbed for his arm, worried for a wild second he'd swing at the man we both hated so much. He simply angled his body in front of mine like he could protect me.

"Masters, if you're throwing your hat in with this prick, you should know a few things. He might have a bigger office and shinier toys, but he takes them and smashes them to pieces. Ask him about his turnover rate. About how many CEOs jump ship after he buys them out because of his single-minded pursuit of money."

Victor's condescending laugh floated over our heads, surely landing among the crowd behind us.

"I think most of my partners applaud the pursuit of money. Isn't that what we're all trying to do here? But, I guess we're on different levels. Take Ava here. A rising star. I really thought she was going to make it but, well." He shrugged pinning me with an evil, satisfied look that made Liam step further in front of me. "One too many items on her to-do list and she's toast. Some people hit their peak early."

"She had a panic attack because she was managing a dozen accounts by herself without any support," Liam growled. "You took advantage of her talent. Wrung out everything she had to offer and demanded more."

Victor rolled his eyes, and Liam jerked. This time, I knew, not to protect me, but to throttle the man.

"Alright." The thought of Liam getting into a brawl with my old boss was enough to free my lost voice. I reached out again, this time clamping my fingers around Liam's arm. "Victor, you've had your fun, played your little game. And now it's time to go."

I stepped around Liam, gesturing to the attendant who had been clutching Victor's jacket, watching the exchange with wide eyes. Him and everyone else, I was sure. Behind me, the party had lulled into hushed whispers. I all but threw the jacket in Victor's face. He swiped it out of the air, flashing a cocky grin.

"I know when I'm not welcome. Nice to see everyone," he wagged his fingers at the room. I refused to give him the pleasure of glancing back to see just how much damage he'd done to our formerly successful cocktail hour. "Don't go too hard on Masters, here. He really did think he was reuniting old friends. Still, it was fun, wasn't it?" He winked at Mark, who furrowed his brow as Victor turned and left.

The sound of the heavy oak door closing behind him echoed through Liam's house. I schooled my face before I whirled, sidestepping Liam as he tried to catch his arm around my waist.

"I need a shot," I called, wafting a hand in front of my face. "Something strong enough to erase the stink of self-entitled asshole we have floating around in here."

A wave of laughter broke over the room, cracking the layer of tension that had settled when Victor walked in.

"I have just what you need, Ms. Anderson." One of the bartenders grinned, already pulling out a bottle of vodka.

"How about one for me, too?" A CEO from one of our portfolio companies urged his date forward.

"Oh, God yes! We all deserve one. Are we trauma-bonded now?"

The last of the awkwardness melted as we crowded around the bar. Had I planned for this to devolve into a rager during the long weeks of planning? Obviously not. But the weirdness of it all called for it.

"Are you alright?" Liam's rough, blunt fingers pulled me away from the knot of people by the bar while infectious, bubbly laughter floated up to the ceiling once more.

"Fine. Where's Masters going?" I glanced over Liam's shoulder in time to see the man slip out the front door.

"He didn't want to stay. Caused enough issues in the few minutes he was here." Liam scowled like he was considering yanking him back inside to give him a piece of his mind. I gripped his lapel.

"Liam, he's our golden ticket to this next raise round. If you chased him out of here, I swear..."

"I didn't. He apparently really did believe we were all old friends and that we'd want to see Victor. He apologized profusely. But I don't want to talk about him. Are you okay?"

"I'm fine. I need a drink, and you need to stop glaring like you want to murder someone."

When I began to back away toward the bar, Liam's hand shot to mine, pressing his fingers to where my palm rested on his jacket, right over his heart.

"I *do* want to murder someone. Victor was out of line and full of shit."

"Yes, obviously. He's always full of shit." My eyes rolled as I tried to pull my hand away. Liam held me tighter.

"Wildes wouldn't be where we are today without you. Not me, or these people, or these opportunities. You are a critical part of this business."

I forced out a laugh. I really wanted that shot. It was bad enough that my old boss, the one I'd pinned all my hopes on, the one who'd dropped me like I was radioactive the moment I'd shown any sign of weakness, turned up on a night like this. I didn't need Liam treating me like I was made of glass, but the interaction with Victor made me sharp and pointy anyway.

"Yeah, well, someone had to send out the invites."

Liam's fingers curled around mine, hard enough to draw my attention away from the bar and back to him. "Don't do that. You know you're not just an assistant. Everyone here knows you run half this damn company. You think I'd let just anyone come in here and do that?" His hoarse, low voice was piercing through, washing away what was left of the icky, inadequate feeling I had whenever I saw Victor. "You are not a failure."

His words, the memory of the last time he said them to me, dripped down my spine like warm honey. My shoulders straightened.

"You're not a failure," he repeated, eyes darting between mine, trying to read something there. "But Victor is. He can't take care of his people, and that's his problem. It was never yours. Understand me?"

"Yes," I responded, because all at once, I did. I had been left out on a ledge at Nexus, dangling higher and higher so Victor could see just how far I'd stick my neck out for him, how much he could get out of me while giving me the fewest resources possible. And I'd fallen so hard, it had taken me years to crawl back to the person I had been before.

But I'd made it, and maybe I was even better now. Because of Liam.

When I'd been at my lowest, he'd given me an opportunity to get back on my feet. More than that, he'd hand-delivered me a clean slate, allowing me to make my own mark on a fledgling organization that frankly had no right to give me the amount of leeway and control I had.

But I couldn't help myself. I loved all of it—the numbers and the strategy and the business and the risk. I loved it as much as Liam did. He'd seen that and held the door open for me, allowed me to walk right in and make myself at home in *his* company, so much so that now it felt like *ours*.

I had worked hard to claw and scratch my way back into confidence today, and I was proud of myself, but Liam had been right behind me every inch of the way, a safe place to land if I fell.

It was the kind of support it would never even occur to Victor to give. With Liam it was just...him.

I wanted to kiss him, right then and there. Looking at him, seeing the concern in his eyes...It went beyond that warm, gooey Dom/sub feeling I got when I was taken care of. It was partnership. Respect. Love.

It welled up, vibrating within me like an electric current. Surely people could *see* this, right? All this light and affection I had for this man was spilling out of every pore.

But they just clinked their glasses and milled around the makeshift bar at the far end of Liam's living room.

"Yes, I understand." I pushed to my tip-toes, brushing a feather-light kiss across his cheekbone. "Master."

He clutched my hand harder to his chest like he wouldn't let me go, but released me when I pulled away.

As a sub, I'd never walk away from Liam like that, teasing and bold. But at work, I wasn't his sub. I was empowered. He had empowered me, and I liked that.

I added an extra sway to my hips knowing he was watching. Because the wetness between my legs was a reminder that as much as I was his, he was mine, too.

"Come wash it all away." Andrea pulled me closer to the bar and shoved a shot glass at me. "I can't believe what a dick that guy is."

"Running you off was the worst mistake Victor will ever make in his life, mark my words." Holmes, bless him, handed me a canapé and wiggled his eyebrows at me.

"Well," I cleared my throat, more than a little overwhelmed by their show of support. I'd spent a long time convincing myself I wasn't cut out for this, that I was broken somehow and the closest I could get to the C-suite was as someone's secretary.

Maybe that was a bunch of bullshit.

"Joke's on Victor. I ended up right where I needed to be."

"Damn straight." Liam reached around me, body brushing against mine, to take a glass from the bartender. We smiled as we threw the drinks down, the smooth burn singeing all the way to my core.

Chapter 12
Liam

"Thank you, sir. Anytime you have another event, give us a call."

I waved the last of the serving staff out the door, shutting off the lights as I made my way back through the house. As well as the night had gone, I was glad to see them leave. I wanted to hear someone else call me sir, but I needed an empty house before that happened. Just one more to go.

"You're sure you're good?" Ben frowned down at Ava. "We can down another shot."

Ava smiled, calm. My cock tightened in my pants.

She was so good at keeping control. Her disproportionate reactions to Victor were some of the only times I'd seen her falter. When we'd run into him last year at a charity event, she'd looked like she wanted to throw up on the nearest philodendron. I couldn't blame her. The man had traumatized her to a truly criminal extent, and the mere thought of it made me want to ram my fist into his smug face.

Except now, tonight, she seemed normal. Unfazed.

She'd frozen up when he'd first walked through the door, but she'd found her spine easily enough. She hadn't just told him to get out; after he was gone, she'd seemed so settled, almost content. It usually took her days to get her cool back after a run-in with her former boss.

I wasn't sure what she'd sorted through or worked out, but it made me want to fuck her through a wall. My girl, my cocky, brilliant girl, was strong. She slayed her own demons and didn't kneel to any man. Except me.

And I wanted it now.

"I'm good," she assured him, tipping a flute of sparkling water in his direction. "If you want to get lit, go for it."

"You don't have to go home, but you can't stay here," I grumbled, leaning against the cabinets. "Bedtime."

Ben groaned at the ceiling. "When did we get old? And boring? I don't know what's worse, the fact that we can't do a shot to celebrate a successful night, or the fact that going home sober actually sounds nice." He kept complaining as he walked to the back of the house where he'd stashed his bags earlier.

Ava tilted her head to size me up. "You stopped drinking at dinner, too. Are you old and boring, Liam?"

I held her gaze, pushing off the cabinets to step closer, nearly brushing against her shoulder. I leaned down to steal a sip of her water. "I never drink before a scene."

Green cat eyes flared, and she swayed closer. I set her flute down with a soft *click*.

"See your boring asses later. Hey, great work today!" Ben was already halfway out the door and didn't stop to notice how I was devouring my assistant with my gaze.

"Bye, Benji," I intoned without taking my eyes off Ava.

Her throat worked. "B-bye!"

"Lock the door on your way out," I requested, waiting to hear the electric lock click into place before I pulled Ava closer.

"You want to do a scene? Right now?" she asked, eyes huge. Her surprise was adorable. Did she really think she'd ask me to kiss her, fuck her, and I'd *wait*?

"Yes." I cupped her head as I lowered my mouth to hers.

Her breath rushed out as our lips touched, and I swallowed it down. This was no tentative, teasing first kiss. I took her mouth the way I'd wanted to since the first day she'd stood in my office, asking for a job she had no business even considering. I kissed her the way I'd wanted to every day since.

I wasn't easy. I was rough and demanding as I swept my tongue inside, pressed against her with a strength I would have held back if it were anyone else. But she wasn't anyone else, and I knew she loved it. She could take it.

She opened, soft and pliant as I crushed her against me, feeling all those curves I hadn't been able to take my eyes off all night. Her taste was better than I'd dreamed. Honey and salt. Something intoxicating I couldn't put my finger on. A whimper escaped her, and I chased the sound, pressing even closer, so hard she stumbled backwards.

I let her go, even though every instinct in my body bellowed for me to follow, to take her to the floor and shove into her tight body until she nearly blacked out with pleasure. I put my palm on her chest when she swayed towards me again, irises blown with desire. My hand slid up to circle her neck.

"You want to play?" I didn't have to ask, but I wanted to hear her say it.

"Yes, Sir."

"Go upstairs. Kneel and wait for me. Shoes off. Scene starts as soon as you walk through the door."

"Yes, Sir."

I watched her ass sway as she padded the stairs, the flex of her thighs as she rose step after step. Finally, when she was out of sight, I let out the gruff sigh I'd been holding in for what seemed like hours. Or years.

I'd waited too long to taste Ava Anderson. I didn't think I could have gone one more day.

I said a prayer of thanks that she hadn't questioned me when I'd told her play started up in my room. Because that kiss? The way I'd sucked on her like she was candy and inhaled her like she was the air I needed to breathe?

That wasn't play. That was just for me.

***

Kneeling on the carpet, arms folded neatly behind her, she was the hottest sight I'd seen in my life. I circled, watching her breath shift her body. Fast. She was excited. As I set a glass of water down on the chest of drawers by the closet, I noticed she'd tucked her black leather pumps underneath. I liked them there.

I liked *her* here.

"Come here, pretty girl." I couldn't wait another second, scooping her up from the floor and walking her over to the bed. She settled in the same position on the dark gray comforter, kneeling and subservient, head down. "You don't need permission to get up here, understand?"

"Yes, Master."

I wasn't sure I could get any harder, but seeing her in here, that *master* so pretty in her mouth, I was going to break a record. Or my zipper.

"You look so good, kneeling here for me." I stroked her face, my thumb catching on her lower lip. "Do you want me to keep you here? In my bed? Command every move you make? Fuck you as many times as I want? You'd like that."

It wasn't a question, I knew it down to my bones. We'd have the time of our damn lives for as long as she was willing to give me.

Heat flooded my veins at the thought. Her, tied down. Legs open for however and whenever I wanted to use her.

"Yes, Master." She sounded breathy, needy. If I slid my fingers inside her the way I wanted to, she'd drip down my wrist. But not yet.

"Take my clothes off."

She kept her head down as she smoothed her hands under my jacket, fingers light and sure. Every whisper of a touch, every time she got closer to ease the jacket off my shoulders or slide my belt through the loops, my heart rate spiked higher.

Her teeth sunk into her lip as my pants gaped open to slide down my legs, cock jutting out of the opening of my boxers. I saw every breath she took, every gasp, flutter, and twitch.

"Do you like what you see?"

"Yes, Sir." Even though her eyes stayed low, I could feel her attention roaming over my skin. That was as much of a turn-on as the thought that my spend was probably still sticky between her legs.

"Your turn." I offered my hand to help her off the bed, watching her body uncoil, bare feet sinking into the carpet. I held her steady as I unzipped her dress, stroking a finger down her spine because she was mine and I fucking could.

"No bra," I commented. I'd been holding on to that little piece of information all night long, the bare expanse of her shoulders doing truly stupid things to my thoughts every time she crossed my path in a sea of investors and business moguls.

"No, Sir." Her dress dropped to the floor, and I spun her to face me. It was a damn crime that I had never seen her breasts before. Full and lush, just enough that they'd spill out the sides of my palms. Her nipples were pert and dusky, begging for my mouth.

"Stop," I ordered, harsh, when her thumbs looped into her underwear. Her hands froze as I bent her backwards, lips closing over the tight little bud of her nipple. I groaned as I sucked on her. The same sound echoed from Ava as her hands threaded through my hair, pulling me closer. I grinned just before my teeth bit into the soft slope, tearing another cry from her as my fingers closed over her wrist, yanking it behind her back.

"Did I give you permission to touch me?"

Her head shook frantically, eyes lowered even as her body shook with desire.

"Get my tie."

She dropped to her knees like a stone, offering it to me like a sacrifice to a god. I jerked her hands above her head, squeezing to let her know to keep them there.

"This isn't for you, Ava." *Lie.* I looped the silk around her wrists, twisting into a knot to bind them together. "You're lucky I'm only tying you up, but you did so well tonight. Did you like it? Traipsing around with my cum underneath your dress?"

"Yes, Sir. Thank you." I wasn't sure what she was thanking me for. Dropping a load between her legs, or letting her off easy for touching me? Probably both. She really was the best little sub. It made my head spin.

"Did it make you wet?"

"Yes, Sir."

"Let's see, then. Keep your hands right here." I hauled her onto the bed, ripping into lace and silk before she could get her bearings.

Seeing her this afternoon, bare pussy flushed and throbbing as she fucked herself with her fingers, had been the last crack to any sort of restraint or sanity I'd had. She was so pretty. Smooth and perfect and pink. I wanted to do vile, depraved things to that little patch of skin and nerves.

"I said I want to see," I snarled, yanking her leg until her foot rested on the mattress, spreading her open. I smacked the inside of her thigh with a *crack*. She moaned, jerking her other leg up so quick, I couldn't even complain that she was making me wait. I slapped it anyway, just to see the pink bloom across her skin. To hear her groan and watch her lift her hips, legs spread to bare her glistening center to me, rimmed with dried white lines of my cum.

"Tell me what you liked about this," I demanded, stroking the traces of my spend on her skin. She swallowed hard as she watched, her legs twitching like she wanted to close them, but she kept herself open for me, just like I'd asked.

"It reminded me I'm yours."

"The sky is blue, too." Her thighs trembled when I slapped them again. "Don't tell me shit I already know, Ava. Tell me what you *liked about it*." I leaned between her open legs, taking her nipple into my mouth again, because I couldn't bear for her to be stretched out like this without my tongue on her.

"I-I'm sorry, Sir. Because..." She stuttered, the great Ava Anderson unraveling under my tongue. I pressed closer, my cock rubbing through her folds, making her arch off the bed. The feeling of her slick heat against me damn near crossed my eyes with pleasure. "Because it felt like you were right there with me all night. Even if you were across the room, I knew you were thinking of me. Paying attention."

"I always am." I shoved against her, sliding so close to where we both wanted me to be. "I loved watching you all polite and polished, knowing as soon as we were alone, you'd be gagging on my cock."

I slid my fingers into that slick wetness that was only getting hotter. My skin was on fire.

"You want that, precious? Want me to shove my dick so far down your throat you can't breathe?"

She moaned, writhing as I petted her, breath coming out in harsh pants. "Yes, Sir. Please."

"Show me." I gave her one last smack between her legs as she scrambled to obey. She practically fell to the floor.

"Good. Open your mouth. Wider." Gripping my tie, I dragged her arms to stretch above her head. The edges of my vision went fuzzy at the sight.

I teased her, tapping the head of my cock against her lower lip, watching her breath come faster and harder until I finally slid inside, moaning at the feel of her wet heat closing around me.

"We'll start slow." My hips pumped softly. I watched, enraptured, as her soft lips slid up my shaft. With her hands bound in mine, she had no leverage, only the sway of her body rocking forward to take me further, a bit more, just a little more...

I flexed in deeper, almost to her edge. I felt her throat spasm and retreated before sliding back in. Again and again, stopping always at the last second before it became too much. Even then, she was full of me, sucking me nearly to the hilt. My head was swimming, the smooth, hot pull of her mouth surrounding my most sensitive flesh as her eyes watered.

I stroked a tear away as it fell. "I want you to take as much of me as you can. You'll do that, won't you? Be a good little girl and gag on my cock?"

She moaned louder, the sound vibrating up my spine and into some previously locked pleasure center of my brain that started melting down as she strained closer, so eager to follow my request that she choked, eyes welling up again.

"I know, baby, but you're doing such a good job. You can take a little more, can't you?" Not much, but it would be enough.

I didn't even have to move. She surged forward to take all of me, coughing. I pulled her arms up even further, backing her off and throwing her off balance.

My grip tightened in her hair with my other hand. I watched as her eyes closed with pleasure even as she fought to force my length further inside her mouth. "You're so eager for me to shove all the way back there, pretty girl? Want it so bad you won't even let me warm you up first?"

Her eyes flicked to mine, usually not allowed, but I'd asked her a direct question, and the answer was written all over her face.

Yes.

My hips surged before I could even think about it, burying inside her until I could feel her throat working around me.

"God...damn..." I groaned, shoving a millimeter closer, watching her face tighten as she struggled to hold me even as she gagged. Her nose brushed against the muscles of my stomach.

I pulled back, watching spit and precum fall in gorgeous strands from her mouth as she gasped for air. I tugged on her wrists, yanking her up to slam my mouth onto hers.

It was violent, all-consuming, as my tongue speared inside. Her still-bound hands fell between us, fingers twitching with the need to feel me. I pulled the edge of the tie, releasing the knot while I angled my mouth better, tasting more.

"Touch me, Ava." Doms didn't beg, but I was close. I wanted to feel her gripping me, grasping as she pulled me closer. Her fingernails pricked my scalp while I shoved my tongue against hers. I didn't let her up for air, and she didn't want it, pressing higher on her toes as I plundered her mouth just like my dick had. I wanted access to every inch, every crevice.

Finally, I couldn't stand any more of the desperate noises mewling out of her mouth, making my dick leak. I whirled, pushing her onto the bed and following close behind, kneeling while she wriggled to close the inch of space between us. I placed a stinging bite over a trail of shooting stars on her ribs I hadn't known were there, hard enough to make her jerk before a groan hissed out of her mouth.

"That's it," I praised, ducking my head to give attention to her right side, her breasts. "Some Doms like their subs meek and quiet. You're good at that, aren't you? Quiet and soft and filling up my head so much it doesn't make sense. But when you're naked underneath me, I want to hear it. I want to make you so out of your mind, every thread of control inside you snaps. I'm your control now. You are just feeling and taste and sound."

"Yes!" Her pitch was nearly a scream as I speared two fingers inside her, testing. She was swollen and hot, so wet I could hear it as my fingers slid in and out.

"Spread your thighs. Wider." It was almost a shame how quickly she obeyed. I would have loved to feel what her cunt did when I spanked her again. But it accomplished what I needed, giving me enough room to work my hand faster, add a third finger. "I feel you clutching my fingers. You want it so badly, don't you?"

"So bad, please. Please,"

Smack.

Her muscles clamped down on my hand as she threw her head back with a silent moan. Perfect. It got her another smack.

"What?"

"Please, Master." Her arms raised, reaching for me. Definitely against the rules, but one look at her face and I knew it didn't matter.

She was gone, flying high on a different plane while she grasped my face, begging me to kiss her, fuck her, make her come. Calling me master and my name and clinging to me like she'd die without me.

Seeing my perfect, polished assistant like this, utterly demolished, ravaged my control. She gasped and whined and begged some more when I slid my fingers out, but I pulled her body closer, looping her leg over my hip.

"Shh, I know what you want, baby. I know…"

"You, Master, please…"

She screamed as I shoved inside until I was buried to the hilt. Her fingernails scraped long streaks down my back as she yelled, arching and rising while I pounded into her like a madman.

It had never been this good, never felt so electric, like it was searing me, branding me with pleasure so I'd never forget it.

She rippled against me as she came apart, screaming as her orgasm tore through her. She was magnificent and the sight of her, feel of her, flooded every one of my senses.

I fucked her harder, jacking her back up when she should have been coming down. But it had been two whole weeks of foreplay and before that, years of wanting.

I cursed, shoving my hand between our thrusting hips to work her clit. She tightened nearly to the point of pain as she screamed again, panting. "Will you come inside me, Master? Please? I want it, I swear I'll be perfect for you, please…"

A raw yell wrenched from my throat. My climax felt like it was torn from the tips of my goddamn toes, spiraling through my body all the way up to my spinning head. I lost track of time, of myself, of everything while I grunted, thrust, emptied inside her body, losing myself in a scene for the first time in my life.

She shrieked as she came again, and both of us were lost. Just feeling and sound and sweat and skin.

Finally, my hips snapped one last time before I collapsed to my elbows on top of her. She made soft, almost pained sounds as she panted, catching her breath.

"Perfect," I told her, gasping, placing soft, pleased kisses across her face. Her eyes drifted closed as she leaned into me wherever my lips fell. "You were so good, Ava. You feel so good I could fuck you again."

I was shaking, seconds from collapsing, but the words felt right. Because I would fuck her again. As soon as my breath and my sanity and my damned *consciousness* returned.

I petted her sweat-slicked skin, murmuring praise and endearments as she came down from her high. After a few moments, when her breathing was even, I pulled away.

She grumbled, reaching for me.

"Hold on." I kissed her lips once, twice, one more time, before I slipped away to the bathroom.

My reflection was a wreck, pink splotches and fingernail marks marring my skin, hair awry and lips swollen. I looked more put together than I felt.

When I returned with a warm washcloth, Ava was sinking into my comforter like she wanted to become one with the Egyptian cotton. She smiled as I took my time, paying attention to the dried marks between her legs. The bites I'd made.

By the time the cloth was in the hamper and the lights clicked off, she hadn't moved an inch. Limp and sleepy, she rolled with me as I pulled her up the bed, tucking her under the covers.

We'd practically slain each other. We were frenzied and manic, and it had wrecked us. And in the aftermath, she curled up against me like a kitten. My heart skipped in my chest.

Aftercare was always fun. A reward for me as much as it was for my subs, but this? This was different. Cozy and soft. I pulled her closer, and she snuggled in tighter. My throat worked.

"Stay the night."

She mumbled something in response, and I pushed her gnarled hair back from her face to see her eyes already closed.

"Please?" I tried again. Her mouth twitched into an almost smile.

"Always, Liam." Long, delicate fingers stroked my skin, right over my heart, as she slipped into sleep.

Chapter 13
Ava

When Liam told me we'd work from the office—rare on a Monday—I'd quietly applauded his strategy. Because since I'd woken up in his bed Saturday morning, sore and sated, I'd been wondering how I'd ever step foot in his house again without dropping to my knees.

He'd been...*everything*. My body was still tingling from the feeling of his hands on me. His mouth. His length between my legs.

And as long as I didn't think about that for too long, or get distracted imagining running my fingertips across his tattoos, everything was fine. Calls went well, meetings churned along, and if we happened to stand a little closer than usual, or catch each other's eyes more often, well, it was Monday, and the office was practically deserted. No one around to see.

"I can finish up the review tonight, and we can get them out first thing in the morning," I told him, clicking through my tablet as he hung up the phone on our last call of the day.

Liam grunted, reminding me of some of the obscene, guttural sounds he'd made when he was inside me. But it was fine. I had made it through today. All I had to do was make it through a few more, until Friday, when I could have him again.

"Ava."

"Hmm?" I asked, gathering my things and thinking about the long shower I could take when I got home. With my fingers and yet another replay of Friday night. The way he'd tilted my head, thrust into my mouth...

"I told myself I wouldn't fuck you again until Wednesday." His words sounded so normal, like he was commenting on his grocery list, it took me a second to really understand them. My laptop landed too hard in my bag as it slipped from my fingers.

"Oh?" I sounded breathless, which made sense considering my heartbeat had just blasted off like a rocket.

"Oh." The word left his mouth on a deep sigh as he leaned back. "And, inconveniently, it's Monday."

"A shame," I murmured, lowering myself into the chair across from him. His hulking desk spread between us, littered with the results of today's work. Reports, sticky notes, various electronics. I should straighten it before I left for the day, but he'd snatched every ounce of my attention with just a few sentences.

"Truly," he drawled, tugging on his lower lip, watching me, talking so quietly I wondered if he'd meant for me to hear his words. "I should have more control when it comes to you."

I placed my folded hands on the mahogany. "You have a lot of control when it comes to me."

His mouth twitched into a grin before he could stop it, his hand spearing into his hair, frustrated or restless or something else entirely. "It would help if you were a little less fantastic, you know."

In bed? At work? As a person? I wanted to know exactly all the ways he found me fantastic. Have him write them out in painstaking detail so I could get it framed and hang it above my bed. Instead of asking, I shrugged. "Sorry."

His smile deepened. "Would you like to go to Dragon with me tonight?"

"Yes, Sir."

He groaned. "Don't call me that here."

"Better take me somewhere I can, then."

As he rose, not bothering to hide the growing bulge in his pants, I could have sworn I heard him mutter something that sounded like "brat" or "fantastic." Possibly both.

***

Liam had worked hard on the way to the club, muttering orders on the phone while his palm slid up and down my thigh in the back of his town car.

Dragon's staff just worked harder.

"Take a look," Liam instructed, sipping his sparkling water as he sprawled in a large leather armchair in the corner of the room. The one he'd chosen for us today, one of Dragon's larger private spaces, was easily three times the size of the space where we'd played on the yoga mat.

It was better-equipped, with a St. Andrew's Cross, along with a spanking bench, and an intimidatingly large iron four-poster bed with various loops and rings studded across the frame. The only other furniture was a small table next to the chair Liam had settled in, likely placed there just for this purpose. For a Dom to sit back, relax, and watch their sub do whatever the hell he wanted.

I licked my lips. I wanted to do a lot. New D/s couples usually eased in slowly, taking time to discover each other's limits and preferences. But Liam had already proven his absolute understanding of my body and what I needed. How much further was he planning to go today?

My attention returned to the bed, looking for a clue. All I found was a dizzying array of toys. A whole collection of floggers—thick-tailed and thin, leather, suede, rubber, weighted at the tip. Vibrators and dildos, butt plugs, cuffs, blindfolds...My gaze flitted across all of it, a kid in a dirty, decadent candy store.

"Pick them up, get a feel for them. The floggers and restraints are mine, but almost everything else I bought for you."

I smiled, weighing one of the smooth, heavy plugs in my hand. "Thank you, Master. They're beautiful." I ran my fingertips across a glass dildo, holding back a frown at its coolness.

"Why don't you bring me your favorites?"

I paused, looking back over my shoulder. A request? "Sir?"

His mouth tilted in a satisfied grin. "You did very well last week, Ava, telling me what you needed, requesting a change. And you felt so damn good."

Ah. A reward then. My smile grew, along with the heat on my cheeks. "Thank you, Sir."

I barely had to look again to snatch up the small flogger. Its thin leather tails would sting, sending pain and endorphins ricocheting around my body. I knelt when I offered it to him, bowing my head before his finger crooked under my chin.

"What else do you like, pretty girl? What other things do you want me to use to make you come apart?" I sighed, nuzzling my cheek into his hand. This was so different from what I expected. Soft and sweet, where last week Liam had been all hard smacks and disapproval.

I brought him a silicon vibrator, the weighted flogger, cuffs, and a small butt plug. He twirled the plug between his index finger and thumb, eyeing me indulgently.

"Done?"

"Yes, Sir." Anticipation clawed through me.

"Hmm," he surveyed the items spread out on the black table. "Any cuts I should know about before we start? Bruising or tenderness?"

"No, Sir." The soreness was gone from our play last week, and his brutal yoga session. He seemed like he was in the mood for something softer today. He stroked my cheek.

"I believe you, gorgeous, but show me anyway? Strip." The word cracked through the room like a lash, his tone tightening my nipples, searing down into my core. I rose, shedding my work clothes methodically until they were in a pile around my feet.

He'd given me permission to look at him earlier, so I watched his eyes as they traveled a leisurely path across my skin, pausing on my breasts, stomach, wrists. The apex of my thighs. I shifted, drenched heat flooding to where he was gazing.

"Stop squirming." His voice was soft, but commanding, as he leaned forward to swipe his thumb through the folds of my bare pussy. I took a sharp breath, willing myself into stillness even though I wanted to press against him, to move my hips against the pressure he put on my aching clit.

"Already wet, darling?" he glanced at me through thick, dark lashes before sucking his thumb into his mouth. "Good."

He stood, grasping my shoulder in firm, confident hands, slotting his thumb into the indent of my collarbone. I nearly groaned at the feeling of his calloused palms against my skin, the sweep of his hands down my arms.

I balled my fingers, trying not to lean into his touch as he swept down my legs until he was kneeling before me. His nose nuzzled the crease of my thigh before gazing up at me.

A shaking quiver started deep in my belly. Because I loved submitting, loved giving over my control. But having Liam Wildes kneel at my feet, looking like he was ready to worship every hair on my head? Indescribably delicious.

"Turn for me," he murmured into my skin. When I obliged, I felt his breath fan against the swell of my butt before the soft graze of teeth made me jolt. Not hard enough to leave a mark, but unexpected. "Steady," he warned, pressing a kiss where his incisors had just been.

He performed the same purposeful perusal of my back, pausing to tap the nodules of my spine, to grip my ass hard enough for my thighs to tremble. His lips pressed into my neck as his thumbs stroked across my straining nipples. "Which do you want tonight? Bed? Bench? The cross?"

"The cross, Sir." I wanted him to string me up and pet me like this until I was a quivering mess.

"Very well. Bench, Ava."

I jerked to a stop, already stepping toward the St. Andrew's Cross. I eyed it for a blank, confused second.

"Is there a problem?" He was still behind me, palming my breasts, but his lazy strokes were getting harder, rougher.

"I...No, Sir."

I hadn't even finished speaking before his fingers tangled in my hair, wrenching my head backwards. All that soft, cozy intimacy was gone now, amber eyes dark and fiery. "Your face says otherwise. Are you confused, precious? Let me lay it out for you." His fingers tightened as he guided me across the room, yanking me up nearly to my toes.

"I've been too easy on you, Ava." He bent me over the bench, lining my body up against the long, padded center support, laying my cheek against the leather. The bench was built like a taller, slimmer picnic table, with two pads on either side for my legs.

I went easily, bending even as my brain struggled to keep up with the change in the scene. No cross? No cuffs? "Our first night, I gave you the mental reprieve you needed. Your punishment last week, you needed that, too, even though you didn't know to ask for it."

"Yes, Sir," I agreed as he folded his fingers over mine, clasping them to two handles on the a-frame supports of the bench. He squeezed before he pulled away, tight enough to hurt.

"This weekend, your eyes were practically begging to suck me off, and I'll admit, I had a lot of fun with that. Didn't you?"

"Y-yes, Sir," I gasped as he ran his hands up the insides of my thighs, pausing to stroke my clit before moving to the other side, pushing my legs up on the pads to spread me wider.

"I know you did. Those sounds you made when you shoved yourself onto my dick..." He trailed off, moaning. His hands smoothed across my back in a firm massage. "But I don't want to start a bad habit of handing you everything you want. I've learned before, Ava. If I give you an inch, you'll take over my whole damn company."

A series of heavy, thudding smacks registered in my ears before I felt them. The light brush of a large, suede flogger. The exact opposite of the sharper, stingier one I'd picked out. It slapped across my skin in gentle circles. "I'm sorry, Sir," I gasped, the feeling far from painful, for now. He was just warming up.

"I don't think you are, actually, and I can't have you forgetting why you're here." Another slap against my thighs, still an easy rhythm, but as he moved the flogger up my legs, towards my ass, my more sensitive skin, I couldn't help but clench my muscles. The flogger abruptly disappeared. "We're not here for you. You're here for me. Relax."

This time, a slap of his hand on my ass-cheek. Nothing as hard as what he'd delivered at the pinnacle of his punishment last week, but enough to jar me even more. He knelt in front of me, face level with mine.

"You don't get to call the shots, do you?"

"No, Sir." *Stupid.* Stupid, stupid for letting him lull me into some hazy, tender fantasy. That wasn't Liam, and it usually wasn't me, either. And maybe I should have been more pissed off that he'd tricked me, but I could already feel myself going pliant over the bench, thinking about how good it was when everything was in someone else's hands and all I had to do was exactly what I was told. "I don't want to call the shots."

"I know you don't, precious. Not here. In here, you're mine. My property, my possession, to do whatever I want with you."

My eyelids lowered in a slow blink. "Yes, Sir," I breathed, finally relaxing against the leather, still cool under my naked skin.

"Good girl," he crooned, sweeping my hair away from my face. "That's it. Eyes on me. I'm going to flog you, because *I* love the flogger. And I'll fuck you, too. Mouth, pussy, ass, that's for me to decide. Do you have any issues with that?"

"I'm yours, Master." All of this had been pre-negotiated, anyway. Our partnership deal had been extensive, and he'd done his homework. He wasn't offering anything even close to my off-limits list.

"Do you have any issues with the toys here tonight? Hard limits, not just a preference," he warned as my attention flitted back to that glass dildo. I only paused a second before settling back into contented complacence. Liam would give me what I needed.

"No, Sir."

He grinned, looking more than a little smug and slightly maniacal as he reared up for a bruising kiss. His tongue speared into my mouth, hot and commanding as I moaned, craning my neck to take more of him. His teeth captured my lip, biting hard enough to sting, to make me want even more.

"Stay," he panted, rising to shuck his shirt, his abdominal muscles rippling as he threw it across the room. "Hands on the bars. Do not move them unless I say so."

"Yes, Sir." I jolted again as another flogger glanced across my back, then another. He had two now, twirling them in constant circles like a figure-eight up and down my shoulders, butt, and thighs. It wasn't the lighter, more needle-y sensation I usually liked, but the longer he went on, bringing awareness to my skin, getting me used to the feel of them, the more I wanted.

My hips squirmed on the bench when he stroked over my thighs again.

"I said still," he barked, thudding the floggers against my ass a little harder this time. I groaned at the taste of that next level, the slightest kiss of pain where the leather hit heated skin. My toes curled. Just like that, the strokes ended, and his feet padded around the bench. "If you can't follow orders, we'll stop. Understood?"

"Yes, Master, I'm sorry, I—"

"Suck." His cock shuttled into my mouth before I could prepare, the feel of his smooth skin over hard muscle the most erotic pleasure. "Harder."

The leather tails landed on my back once more, first on one side of my spine, then the other. My inner muscles clenched, squeezing as my neck twisted to take more of him, deeper.

The leather fell, picking up speed in time with his thrusts. It was overload, it was good and bad and an emptiness between my legs I was desperate to fill. But the only thing that mattered was him, his flesh against mine, making it good for him because he'd asked me to. I rolled my tongue, hollowing out my cheeks.

"Excellent, Ava," he praised, smacking leather further down before pulling back. I gasped, saliva dripping from my lips as he walked away, dick still hard and jutting out of his pants.

Thwack. I jerked, the tails hitting right at the apex of my thighs where I wanted them most.

"Are you still with me? I want to go harder."

"Yes, please, Master." I barely stopped myself from offering my hips up, but I still must have shifted. The leather smacked my butt once, twice, three times. He was just using one now. Harder, more targeted strokes now that I was ready.

"I said." *Smack.* "Hold." *Smack.* "Still." *Smack.* This time the flogger cracked across my thighs, making me whimper and groan. It hurt so *good,* and I knew there was more. He could give me more. If I was just good enough for him.

"Can I go harder?" he asked, his fingers brushing my sensitized skin. I nearly jerked at the gentle touch, expecting the slap of leather again, but he was disorienting me, standing behind me so I couldn't see where he was, didn't know where his next strike would land.

I groaned when his hand slipped down to feel the swollen skin between my legs.

"You're soaked," he muttered, almost to himself, canting his fingers in and out as my muscles spasmed, clutching like I could pull him in further by sheer force of will. "I'm going to fill you here while I hit you. Send you to the moon with this pussy stuffed full."

"Master, please," I gasped again, this time holding perfectly still because if I didn't get another hit, I was going to— "Ah!" A hard chill between my legs. The glass.

He teased the tip up and down my clit. I clamped down on every muscle in my body to avoid jerking away from the cold sensation. "I love the glass." Without warning, he tilted the toy to slide inside me. I was so wet, so ready, it slipped nearly all the way in with a single push. I whimpered again at the foreign feeling, willing myself into stillness.

"No give, no softness." He moved it in and out. Seconds ticked by, minutes, and it warmed between my legs. "You have to work for it."

He shoved it deeper, harder. A sharp exhale escaped my body. It almost felt...nice.

"The trick is," he reached again to stroke the sensitive nerves between my legs. Oh, *oh that was good*. I moaned, struggling to keep from moving my hips as an orgasm sparked on the edges of my consciousness, only to stop short when the dildo slipped a few inches.

"The trick is," he repeated, still playing with my clit. His other hand stroked the sensitive skin of my ass, and I realized he wasn't holding onto the glass at all. "that the glass toys are most effective, in my opinion, if you don't use them for pleasure. But for *focus*."

He tapped the base of the toy with his finger, the dull vibration skittering up my spine as it inched inside me once again.

"Another thing I've learned," his voice circled the bench. The tips of the flogger trailed in a slow sweep up my spine until he stopped in front of me, his cock mere inches from my lips. "is that you do best with a task. Hold it in, Ava."

As the flogger hit my ass with a weighty *slap*, every muscle in my body constricted. I could feel the dildo inside me, every minuscule shift and wobble. The flogger fell again, landing in quick succession on my back and thighs.

I squeezed the handholds, eyes shut. My thighs shook, but the bench held me open, and Liam held no room for mercy, the leather slapping almost continuously.

"Should I stop?" he demanded when I shuddered, a tear rolling down the bridge of my nose.

"No!" I cried, breath heaving, because I needed more. The rush of pleasure-pain was zipping through my skull. "Please, Master, no."

"You're close," he assured me, the flogger landing across my shoulders, making me cry out. "So close, precious. You wanna fly?"

He kept talking, a litany of praise and filthy commentary and requests and accusations as the leather hit my skin. My world shrunk. I diminished into only touch, heat, gasping cries.

He fisted my hair, tightening as the hits rained down, and between one strike and the next, I flew.

The euphoric sensation flooded my brain, the pain shifting suddenly to the most heavenly pleasure. A long groan echoed around the room. Me, I distantly realized as my head fell forward, supported only by Liam's grip on my hair. My fingertips buzzed and tingled, clit bumping against the leather of the bench as I lost that iron-clad control of my hips.

"Yes," Liam hissed, wrenching my head up to see my face. I loved it so much. The release, the endorphins, the way he made me feel safe enough to do this. A bright, stunning grin lit his face. "I know you do, precious. I love it, too. You're doing so good. Look at you."

The flogger hit the ground, and I whined when he left my line of sight, only for his hand to stroke against my abused back.

"I'm right here. Right here, I just have to feel this...dammit, Ava, you're dripping, I can't..."

I screamed when he pulled the toy from between my legs. It felt like it was part of me now, integral to this incredible high rushing through my veins. But one second I was empty and the next, Liam was *there*, shoving inside as my body grasped desperately around his cock, frantic.

"Holy..." he groaned, his balls slapping against my clit as he shoved in and out with hurried snaps of his hips. "*Yes,* Ava. You feel like heaven. I can feel you sucking me in, wanting me deeper, wanting..." he trailed off on a long moan as I tried to move my hips with his, match his rhythm.

He couldn't be deep enough, hard enough.

"Liam, please. I can't..." I felt like I couldn't breathe, even as I sucked air into my lungs in big bursts. Everything was hot and too much and not enough.

"I know, baby. Hold on." His fingers dipped down to find my clit while he rocked in and out at a frenzied pace.

And I was gone. I'd thought Liam had given me my best last weekend, but I'd been an idiot. A fool. Because nothing, *nothing*, compared to this. I screamed and jerked and moaned. Time didn't exist anymore, just feeling. Just Liam behind me, shuddering with his own pleasure. Just the heat still radiating from my back. The waves of endless ecstasy roaring through me.

Everything went black or flashed gold or rainbows or something. All I knew was one minute I was in the throes of a magically, cathartically, soul-stoppingly incredible orgasm, and the next, I was still, breathing heavily as I drifted back into my body. Liam's hands were soft on my back, stroking all the places where the flogger had landed.

I let out a long sigh.

"You with me, precious?"

I groaned, hardly able to open my eyes as he rounded the table. He sifted through my hair, fingers rubbing light circles across my aching shoulder blades. I would have gladly given my entire stock portfolio for him to never stop. "You need a rubdown. Some oil. Water." His finger circled my bottom lip. I grinned.

"Cuddles," I murmured.

"Cuddles," he agreed, his voice closer. When I fluttered my eyes open, he was right in front of me, staring down with that tenderness from before. My heart fluttered, too. That part hadn't been a trick.

"Ava?"

"Mmm?"

"You can let go of the handles now."

I pried my fingers loose, joints aching from where they'd gripped so tight. I let my hands drop to dangle towards the ground, as limp as the rest of me.

Chapter 14
Liam

"Gross, no one told me there'd be kids here," I scowled, pretending to gag as I stepped aboard the massive yacht.

"Uncle Liam!" My seven-year-old niece, Callie, dropped her crayons to run at me.

"Callie-Cat." I scooped her up as she leaped into my arms.

"Look at our boat! It's *huuuuge.*" She wasn't wrong. Together, we looked at all the opulence around us. Big galley kitchen, multiple bedrooms, and an open-concept deal that didn't seem capable of having a bad view of the harbor.

I whistled. "Well, your dads know how to go big."

"Hey, ten-year anniversary is a big one. What's the point of you making my husband work his butt off for all this money if we can't rent a floating mansion for the weekend?" My brother, Tommy, slung his arm over Ben's shoulder, smacking a kiss on his cheek.

"First of all, keep your hands off my business partner, or I'll really throw up," I grinned as I handed over a bottle of Dom Pérignon. "Second of all, congratulations or whatever."

"Such a softie," Ben tsk'ed, handing the bottle off to a woman passing by with a crew uniform on. "But I know your salary, Liam, you could have sprung for a whole case."

"You should be buying *me* champagne. I'm the reason this ever happened in the first place." Taking credit for Ben and Tommy's relationship was one of my purest joys in life. Ben and I had hit it off from almost the first day of our intro to finance class in college. It hadn't taken long for us to start talking seriously about making our own firm where we could do things on our own terms. When Tommy had come down to visit me one weekend and the two had met, it was one of those crazy sparks flying, first-sight kind of deals.

I grinned smugly down at Callie. "You and your brother wouldn't even exist if it weren't for me."

Her face screwed up. "Would this boat exist?"

I glanced around the sleek leather and plexiglass monstrosity. "Um, probably."

"It has a captain and everything, and he knows how to drive it," my niece rambled, unconcerned that the fate of her existence had once rested in my nineteen-year-old hands.

"Well, that's a relief. I don't know anyone else who could figure out how to drive this thing."

"Auntie Ava could," she told me seriously.

"Probably true, yes," I responded, just as grave.

"Let's not try to find out, alright?"

Ava sauntered through the galley with my three-year-old nephew, Wyatt, in her arms. Underneath her crocheted cover-up, she had on a red bikini that I needed to see more of. That see-through material wasn't see-through *enough*.

"Liam." She nodded as she passed, on her way out the big sliding doors to the bow of the ship where Wyatt was pointing and babbling excitedly.

"Ava," I drawled, letting Callie wriggle from my arms to follow them, joining in with her brother's chattering. A family function wasn't a great place to ogle my secretary, but that getup looked good on her.

Just not as good as she'd looked at the club last night, nearly passed out from a long session with a lovely set of nipple clamps and a vibrator.

I dragged my eyes away from her ass, willing myself not to think about how she'd tasted, sounded, *felt* underneath me. It had been three weeks since we'd abolished the no sex rule. Even though I'd allowed myself to call her twice outside of our Friday meetings, it wasn't enough.

I was addicted, and no matter how much I'd tried to brace myself for the fall, nothing could prepare me for how utterly and completely she'd captured my thoughts, my heart. Loving Ava from afar was bad enough, adoring her up close was going to kill me.

She matched me, step for step. She made me laugh, her irreverent confidence the strongest aphrodisiac I could imagine. And in bed, when she submitted to me, it felt like being handed some golden, rarefied achievement. My chest puffed up just thinking about it. She was just...perfect. Everything I wanted. It wasn't even that hard admitting to myself that I loved her. That, maybe, I'd loved her this whole time.

The sound of a smack and a yelp broke my reverie (and my focus, still on her ass).

"What the hell, Tom?" Ben rubbed his chest, glaring at my brother.

"You didn't tell me," Tommy nodded in my direction and sipped on a glass of champagne the server brought around. Ben sniffed as he took a flute, as well.

"Unsubstantiated."

Tom's eyebrow twitched. "I think we can substantiate now. The poor boy is practically drooling."

"If you could stop talking about me like I'm not here, that would be great," I cut in, forcing a smile at the server as I took my own glass.

I didn't want to make a big deal out of what Ava and I had. Not when it was just...

And that's what stumped me. What we were doing was way more than sex. The trust between us, the edges we pushed, the intimacy. It even went beyond the traditional Dom/sub relationship, and I wasn't sure what to do about it.

In the end, it didn't matter how cool I tried to play it. Tommy threw his head back and cackled so loudly that Ava glanced up from the front of the ship where the wind whipped dark locks into her face.

"Keep. Your voice. Down." I grumbled, downing my champagne in a single swallow. I'd need stronger stuff if my brother was going to act like an ass.

"We've been waiting for this for about three years. It's a big day for us." Ben clicked his glass against Tom's. Traitors, both of them.

"It's not what you think," I insisted. Where was that server? I needed a refill.

"It's exactly what we think. Oh, this is the best anniversary present I could think of." Tom rested his cheek on top of Ben's head. "The kids already call her auntie. I'll be so happy to make it official."

My heart tried to take a running leap out of my chest. "Hold on, you two are way ahead of yourselves—"

"When do you think she'll propose?" Ben wondered aloud. An image of Ava in a white dress grated on my mind. Then my brain flipped it to a black silk number, and that clicked into place for me. All our friends and colleagues. A big bash on a rooftop somewhere. Taking her home after work. Giving her my name.

Fuck, I was so fucking fucked.

"Hopefully soon. Liam deserves a big fat rock after all the waiting around he's done."

The server reappeared as Ben shot champagne out of his nose, the two of them giggling like idiots. I sighed, glancing back at Ava, wishing she was here to bash their heads in. She was looking at us with a question in her eyes, but I shook my head. I wasn't willing to expose her to this yet. She was so strong and so skittish. I didn't need anything to spook her away from what we were building. I grabbed another flute, tipping it in Ava's direction, asking if she wanted any.

She scrunched her mouth to the side like *what do you think?*

"Unsubstantiated, my ass," Tommy finished chuckling, graciously allowing the server to top off his wine. "Right, they're totally *not* looking like they want to climb into each other's skin."

"Do you think they finally realize they're the exact same person with the same crippling drive to succeed and an identical love of money and good scotch?" Ben chimed in.

"Okay, bye, lunatics." I grabbed my freshly filled champagne and beat a hasty retreat over to the front of the ship. I whirled at the last minute before opening the doors. "And I swear to God if either of you breathes a word of this to Ava, I will end you. Fired. Disowned. You hear me?" I pointed at them, glaring daggers.

Tommy's mocking smile turned soft. "You know we just want you to be happy. I think she's good for you."

"Yeah, well...Me, too."

By the time I made my way across the deck of the ship, we were underway. Before Ben, Tommy, and the kids set sail for three days to live out their yacht life fantasies, they'd graciously decided to share the experience for a day with their "extended family." I hadn't bothered to point out that I wasn't extended, and Ava wasn't family. I was just happy to relax with my favorite people in a place where I could realistically claim not to have Wi-Fi access.

I needed a damn break.

"What was that all about?" Ava asked, taking a sip of wine.

"Don't worry about it." I didn't deign to look inside, knowing full well that Ben and Tommy were probably watching our exchange like vultures desperate for any scrap of gossip they could get. "Hey, happy boat day."

Our glasses clicked together.

"With limited cell service." She waggled her eyebrows.

"Ooh, baby. Full-time chef, too." Pleasure melted across her face, and she looked happy enough for me to consider renting one of these things next weekend just to take advantage of the privacy.

"Ah!" A beach ball flew straight into her face. I couldn't help the laugh that busted out of me as she bobbled her wine and the ball. I popped it out of her hands and sent it sailing back to my niece and nephew, where they passed it back and forth over a row of lounge chairs.

"You cretins!" she called, shoving her flute at me. "Hold this. I need to kick some tiny ass at beach ball tennis."

"I think it's just called volleyball, babe!" I yelled at her retreating form, a smile stretching my mouth as I admired her backside in that little cover-up again.

Grinning outright, admiring even more, when she turned around and stuck her tongue out at me.

***

We spent the day on the water, splashing around in the boat's floating pool, throwing the kids in until our arms were sore. Eating, drinking. Laughing so hard Ben nearly choked on a lobster roll.

As much as I wanted to haul Ava into the nearest bathroom and strip her little bikini off, the day wore on, and I contented myself with quick, innocent touches, thinking less and less about sex and more and more about *her*.

I'd known she fit into my business, but seeing her here, relaxed and happy, reminded me how well she fit into my *life*. She chatted with my parents when they called to wish Ben and Tommy a happy anniversary. She spearheaded the kids' water gun attack and snuck them candy when she thought no one was looking.

As the marina came into view, I realized I'd been missing out. I'd spent so long telling myself it was enough for her to be my partner at work, my friend, that I didn't need to ask her for more. But now that I had a taste of her, I understood I'd never be fully satisfied unless I had every piece.

Not just workdays and Friday nights, but weekends. Mornings. Every day. With our friends or alone in my house. Arguing about clients, then screwing till we passed out. Going to dinner or the office or nowhere, as long as we were together.

She joined me on the bow as the boat docked, dropping us off so Ben, Tommy, and the kids could head back out to sea for a few nights of family vacation. She was quiet, like me, watching the waves lap against the sides of the ship.

Behind us, Ben and Tommy argued with Callie and Wyatt about a second helping of dessert. The servers flitted around, securing things and cleaning up dishes and no one was paying us a speck of attention.

Fuck it.

I wrapped my arm around her waist, nearly sighing when she leaned into me.

We stayed like that, wrapped up in each other, content for the world to pass by, but I could feel our time ticking down. Soon, they'd lower the plank. She'd go to her place, and I'd go to mine, and it would be empty and cold, and I'd lay awake all night wishing she was there.

What a pathetic waste that would be, when she could be with me. When I should be able to reach over and stroke her skin whenever I wanted to. Make her hot and horny, bring her up and back down again. We were good at that. We would be good at all the rest of it, too.

"Come home with me," I murmured.

She hummed, considering, but she didn't pull away. "For a scene?"

The captain called something down to the crew, and I resisted the urge to draw her closer. To tell her she *was* getting in my car and that she *would* let me strip that bikini off her when we got home. Because I didn't want a scene.

"Just...to come home with me. For the night."

"Just for tonight, huh?" She leaned her head back to look at me, eyes twinkling as a wry smile stretched her lips.

For all the nights. I kissed her nose. "Something like that."

We hugged the kids goodbye and studiously ignored the looks Ben and Tommy gave us as I led Ava off the boat and into my town car. Once the doors closed behind us, she leaned into my side, watching the city outside like it was a dream.

It felt like one. Her and I, not going to work, not going to the club. Somewhere in the middle. My thumb brushed lazy circles on her thigh, playing with the hem of the skirt she'd changed into when the sky started going dark.

We held the calm, quiet bubble around us as I led her into the house. The door was barely closed and locked before she was on me, dragging my mouth to hers at the same time I pulled her hips into mine. We kissed like we had seconds left to live, desperate and hungry, sharp where the rest of the day had been so calm and comfortable.

I bit her lips, licking inside as she clutched at my head. Something had shifted, changed, flooded everything I thought I'd known, burying it beneath everything that was *her*. I wondered if she felt it too. She had to have, the way her leg twined around mine as I boosted her up and backed her against the wall.

A picture frame rattled as I shoved her against it, pinning her hips with mine. "It's a shame you aren't wearing that little red bikini anymore," I rumbled, tongue darting between her teeth.

"You liked that?" she gasped, wrapping her arms around me as if I wasn't already almost as close as I could get to her.

"Want to know how many times today I thought about cornering you in a bathroom and shoving them aside?"

She groaned, her head falling back with a thud as I bit down the column of her neck. "I'd have liked that."

"I know you would, dirty girl. But we had to play nice."

"Dirty girl? Not pretty?" Her nimble fingers flew across the buttons of my shirt while I shoved her skirt up to her waist.

"You're only a pretty girl when we play. When that's all you want to be." I fumbled with my zipper, working to keep her upright while I pulled her underwear to the side.

"The rest of the time I'm not pretty?" She gasped as I slid against her soaking lips, grinding into the warmth I found there.

"The rest of the time..." *You're mine.* I shoved inside and she arched against me, crying out at the invasion. My walls melted, every concern and hesitation obliterated in the face of the way she felt against me. *With* me. "The rest of the time you're *everything.*"

I pounded into her, desperate, gasping and groaning. I slammed my mouth onto hers, tongue and teeth clashing as I speared inside over and over and over, roaring when I felt her tighten around me.

She threw her head back and screamed, pulling the pleasure from the depths of my soul, whimpering as I jerked and spilled inside her.

We panted against each other's lips, cocooned in the darkness, the sounds of the city just outside.

I groaned, pulling out of her and stumbling on unsteady legs as I grabbed for her hand. "Bed."

I wasn't sure if it would be to sleep or to get a second round under way. I just knew I needed her there.

After she sent me back downstairs for her bag and demanded a spare toothbrush, Ava starfished on top of me, smiling and satisfied. I watched the slow spin of the fan above us, stroked her, and wondered if I'd ever been this content in my life.

"We should get a boat." Her whispered words caught me just as my eyes started to blink closed, and she surprised a laugh out of me.

"We should get a boat I can fuck you on whenever I want." My lips pressed against her forehead, and she snuggled closer.

"I'll have to learn how to drive it for real then, so it can be just the two of us. Don't want those pretty little servers walking in." She yawned as her eyes blinked shut. "Don't want to share you."

I brushed the hair off her cheek. "I don't want to share you, either."

Chapter 15
Liam

My fingers patted around the bedside table. It took a few tries, but eventually I palmed my phone and snoozed the alarm, nearly yanking it out of the wall as I rolled back into bed. Back to the warm body hogging my covers.

"Ugh, is there ever a single moment when you're not violent and depraved? You sound like a herd of a thousand elephants just turning your alarm off," Ava complained, frowning even harder when I pulled her out of the little burrow she'd made on her side of the bed.

Her side. Might as well give it to her, since she'd taken up space there almost all weekend. Her phone buzzed on its charger on the other bedside table and her little red bikini was wadded up somewhere in the sheets.

Two nights and a whole day, and we'd barely managed to venture out for food and water. I wasn't ready to face the reality of a workday, or the rest of the world. Not when I wanted to stay right here, with her, on the little patch of my mattress she'd staked a claim on.

Was it really this easy? She'd fitted herself into my business nearly from day one. Who was to say she couldn't just slot herself into my life, into the blank space that I hadn't realized was there? One that seemed perfectly Ava-shaped, when I really thought about it.

"Don't exaggerate. Two hundred elephants, tops."

She grumbled, grouchy and sleepy, when I drew her even closer. Ava was not a morning person at the best of times, and I'd kept her up late last night.

"It feels like you're more into the Dom/sub relationship you have with your nightstand. I know you like whacking it around like that." She finally stopped resisting, letting me draw her all the way into my arms. Her cheek nestled into the indent of my shoulder. Next to my head, my phone started buzzing with irregular messages and notifications, waking up for the day.

But all of that could wait.

"If you're jealous, babe, just say so," I teased, brushing my lips against hers. If we kept it quick, showered fast, we could still have some fun before we stumbled into my downstairs office to start the day's meetings. And hell, maybe we'd end up having some more fun in there, too.

We'd said our physical relationship wouldn't overlap with work, but something had changed over the last few days. Something bone-deep and foundational. We'd need to talk about that. Maybe after the shower.

"Helllll no, absolutely not." Ava jerked backwards to evade my kiss. "I have morning breath." Her last words were muffled against the sheet as she tried to scooch to the edge of the bed.

"Me, too. Does that cancel out?" I managed to get my hands around her waist and haul her back to me, with her kicking and squirming the whole way. She screeched when I yanked the sheet down and huffed into her face.

"You disgusting asshole, get off of me!" She struggled to roll away again, but everywhere she moved, I was there, pinning her in. This was the most fun I'd had on a Monday morning, ever.

"Come on," I cajoled, taking a second to feel her up when her breasts and my hands crossed paths in the impromptu wrestling match. "Let me kiss you."

"No. Until you brush your teeth, and I brush mine, your mouth is getting nowhere near me."

Well, now. That sounded like a challenge, and I never backed down from one of those. "Do I need to brush my teeth to eat you out?"

She stilled just as I pressed her down, splaying her thighs open. I could practically hear her brain spinning as she glared at me. She rolled her eyes as I grinned back. "I suppose we could come to an agreement," she allowed.

Her phone vibrated again on the other side of the bed.

"Do me a favor and put that back on Do Not Disturb while you can still feel your fingers." I swooped down to steal a kiss while she was distracted, laughing while she sputtered and bucked, knowing there was no possible way she could get away from me.

"Promises, promises." I heard her mutter just before I disappeared underneath the comforter. Her body twisted underneath mine as she reached to silence her phone.

"Good girl," I whispered against her ribs, feeling her shiver as I licked her nipple, nuzzling the heavy curve of her breast.

"Liam."

"Shhh, baby, I'm doing something." My tongue circled her belly button, savoring the smooth feel of her skin under my lips.

"*Liam*." Her tone stopped me from going any further. *Shit*. I rolled to my knees as she sat up, clawing the covers away, ripping us out of the soft cotton into the harsh light of Monday morning.

She shoved my phone in my face, already bringing hers to her ear as she stood and strode across the room. I didn't even have time to enjoy the view, sucked into the steady buzz of notifications, the never-ending list of missed calls from the night before. Investors and partners and CEOs and even Ben, who was supposed to be offline on a yacht with his perfect little family.

I got the gist after scrolling for a few seconds, a picture forming from multiple texts and voicemail transcripts from worried investors. A bar brawl, shattered windows, two people in the hospital.

And Mark Masters at the center of it all, in police custody because of the gram of cocaine he'd had in his pocket.

I was dialing Ben before my feet hit the ground.

***

"Have I apologized enough yet?" I asked, rubbing gritty eyes as I leaned back in my desk chair.

"Unless you're the one who planted the coke on him, there's nothing for you to apologize for."

"Maybe just a general 'sorry this dickhead was such a dickhead and severely damaged his reputation and possibly tanked his company's valuation just as we were looking to buy it? All while you're on vacation?'"

Ben paused. I could hear the kids laughing and screaming in the background. "On second thought, I'll accept that."

My doors slid open, and Ava strode in. In our rush to leave the house this morning to do as much damage control as possible, she hadn't been able to stop at her place. She'd done a decent job piecing together an outfit with one of my button-downs, a belt, and the skirt she'd worn home from the boat Saturday. Any other time, the whole effect of her walking around in my clothes with no one the wiser would have had me on my knees, but there wasn't any time for that.

Not with partners ringing the phone off the hook, freaking out about risk assessments and demanding to know what we were going to do about VestedAI. Everyone knew the technology was the game-changer, but Masters had just blown everything up in his own face.

Fucking Masters.

Half our partners wanted us to swoop in and grab the company before anyone else could—to hell with the risk. The other half were threatening to pull from the next funding round if we had anything to do with the man.

As she came closer, I could see Ava's face glowing with a flush of adrenaline and that insane high we got when a deal went our way. "What do you have, Anderson?" I asked, tipping forward in my chair as her mouth curled into a satisfied grin. My heart thudded in my chest.

"I've got it."

"Thank God," Ben sighed over the speakerphone. Green cat eyes narrowed in on me.

"I got Masters on the phone. He's out on bail and coming here now."

"He's coming straight here from a night in jail?" I'd at least have stopped for a shower.

"He knows he's screwed. He's ready to sign a contract right here, right now."

"The investors are going to go apeshit—" I started, snapping my mouth shut when she held up her hand. She had a crazy predatorial look that shouldn't have been hot in the middle of a crisis like this, but still made me want to bend her over my desk.

"He says if we buy him out, he'll step down as CEO, effective today. He takes the fall, saves the company from bad press. We get the tech." Triumph flashed in her eyes. I stared at her, dumbfounded.

"He's willing to do that?"

She shrugged, nodding at the phone in her hand. "That's what he says. This company is his baby, and he's spinning out. I say we do it."

"Yeah, Vested *is* his baby," Ben sounded skeptical. "Do we really think he's going to let it go this easily?"

Ava frowned at the phone as if she could make him feel her disapproval across the line.

"We sign the deal of the century, boot him on his ass. It looks like we're in control, taking the reins."

I spun my chair back and forth as I considered it. "It would miraculously make all the investors happy. Distance ourselves from cocaine guy while we get to snag Vested."

"We..." Ben trailed off, thinking, too. "We could probably offer less money. The valuation is tanked, and Masters knows that. This could be our opportunity to get this thing for a steal."

My attention flew back to Ava. "Are we ready for that? Due diligence, everything buttoned up?"

For a split-second, so fast it could have been my imagination, her lips tightened before smoothing into a confident smile. "Yes. Yeah, I say we do this."

"Ben?" I asked without taking my eyes off her. She looked back, steady.

"We haven't gotten this far by playing it safe. If Ava says it's a go, let's go."

She looked at me expectantly, and the silence on Ben's side of the call grew heavy, too. All signs pointed to...yes. Would it be the craziest cowboy-style sale of the year? Hell yeah, and part of me liked the way it could all go down. Us on top. Everyone else wondering how the hell we'd pulled it off.

But something about Ava...

She leaned her hands on my desk, eyes glinting so brightly I could read her mind. *Come on, Wildes. Let's do this.*

"Fuck it, let's bag a bargain business."

Ava cheered, already scurrying out of my office. "I'll make the calls. We'll have it all set up as soon as he gets here. Conference room, thirty minutes. Let's close it."

She was practically buzzing as the door swung shut behind her.

"I should retire. An old guy like me can't keep up with all this," Ben muttered.

"We're the same age."

"I'll save you a spot at the home, grandpa."

"Yeah...yeah." I shoved a hand through my hair, an uneasy cocktail of uncertainty and adrenaline coursing through my veins. The day had started out crazy and hadn't gotten any better. I should have felt good, settled about the decision we'd all made. We'd get the company and get Masters out of our hair. It was a win-win.

"Liam, you good?"

My gaze strayed to the doors Ava had just walked through, practically levitating from the coup she was about to pull off. Maybe this was just the thing—the big win—she needed to realize how much she brought to the table.

"I'm great. I'll call you in thirty when Masters is here."

The silence of my office pressed against my ears long after the line went dead.

Chapter 16
Liam

Masters's black eye could probably be seen from space. It was definitely visible to all my employees staring through the glass as he plopped his ass into one of our conference room chairs.

"You're late," I droned, head propped on my fist. Ava shot me an arch look that would usually make me stand down, but Masters had been giving us nothing but headaches since day one. Even though he was about to sign a contract with a laughably smaller valuation than we'd been discussing just yesterday, the way he looked walking in here—tired and beat up, but content—set me on edge.

I wanted this deal done. Now.

"I had a tough night; cut me some slack." He closed his eyes against the fluorescent lights.

"How about we just cut you a check and you go on your merry way?" I offered.

"Yeah, let's get this done and you can take a little breather, Mark." Ben sounded fine through the speakerphone. It seemed like he really had banished any of the hesitation he'd voiced back in my office. That made one of us.

Masters's expression flickered with something like relief before his mask slipped back into place. He didn't look at me as he grabbed a pen from the middle of the table. "I'll sign anything you want. I just want this over."

The sag of his shoulders, the sigh in his voice…everything about him triggered every instinct I'd honed over the last decade building Wildes.

"A little eager, aren't we?" I dug in. "You built VestedAI from the ground up. Usually, we get more pushback from executives when we snatch their life's work out from under them."

"Though we're all aware of what a sacrifice you're making. Really, the best choice for everyone," Ava forced a grin in Masters's direction before aiming a narrowed, twitching glare at me.

My jaw clenched. No matter how much I wanted to just go with this and make her day, maybe her year, I couldn't shake the feeling that something wasn't right.

"We're only waiting for the last of the updated paperwork to come out of legal. They're pushing it through at lightning speed." She settled into a chair between me and Masters. "While we wait, I was hoping you could shed some light on some of the recurring revenue numbers and registered users. We keep coming up against a discrepancy, and I'm sure it's just an error on our end."

She shuffled neatly through the stack of folders in front of her, probably every report and document that had been generated on VestedAI in the last twelve months, all perfectly organized, alphabetized, and ruthlessly bent to her will.

Or not. My chair swiveled in her direction. "You're still having issues with the numbers? You said we were good."

"We are." She clipped, barely looking up. "I just want to clarify a few things before we sign on the dotted line."

"If things still aren't adding up with the finances…" Game over. I didn't care how compelling this deal was. My gut was telling me to bail, and this was the last straw. If Ava wasn't one hundred percent sure, all this was a nonstarter.

"No!" Masters leaned further in his chair, running a hand through his stringy hair. "Everything you need is in the documents we sent over." He spared Ava a withering look before bypassing her entirely to address me. "If she's having trouble with it, maybe you need to give it to someone a little more qualified."

Ben's breath sucked in over the speakerphone.

"Excuse me?"

Masters blanched at my tone before he rolled his eyes, a sneer settling over his features. "I know you've taken a liking to her," he paused. The implication in his voice made me want to ball my fists and put them through his face. "But it's obvious she can't even decipher simple financial statements. Maybe she can get us some coffee or something, and you and I can discuss this like gentlemen."

I leaned back in my chair, cocking my head to look at him from a different angle. Maybe he'd look like less of an asshole. "Gentlemen?"

"Yes," Masters sounded confident. My voice, softer now, must have lulled him into some sense of security. His shoulders softened. "We both know this is a man's business."

"Hmm." I stroked my chin, glancing at Ava. "If you were a man, what would you tell me about the discrepancies with VestedAI's recurring revenue numbers?"

A muscle feathered across her jaw, her mouth turning down in annoyance or disappointment or...something. "I'd tell you there's a mismatch between annual revenue, registered users, and active accounts."

"Uh huh. So, as a man, I'll ask you, *as a man*," I turned back to Masters. "What's wrong with your numbers?"

A vein popped on his forehead, drawing my attention to the tiny beads of sweat forming on his hairline. "Nothing. There's nothing wrong with them. We...we gave you everything you asked for and re-worked it six ways to Sunday when your idiot secretary couldn't make heads or tails of it." He glared at Ava like *she'd* been the one to clap him in cuffs last night. "I know you call her the COO but she's an assistant for God's sake, Wildes. Come on, what are we doing here? You're going to hinge the biggest deal of your life on what your secretary tells you?"

His harsh, almost panting breaths reverberated around the conference room. Three or four people huddled outside, clutching papers and tablets and waiting to barge in here in a flurry of activity. I raised my hand, holding them off while I took in the pandemonium of the office through the glass. People scurried around, someone from finance outright ran through the cubicles.

Masters had done this, turned my usually well-ordered operations into a circus. And Ava...Ava just sat, rigid, staring at the pile of papers in front of her, anger and shame clashing across her features.

Yeah, fuck that.

"Deal's off."

There was a beat of silence before Ben muttered a curse. I could only hope someone on that fancy boat of his had brought him a drink. I'd need one after all this, too.

"What?" Masters sounded like I'd just kicked him in the nuts, which...maybe I had, in a way.

"Off. Feel free to see yourself out. Have fun cleaning up your shit-storm by yourself. We won't be taking that on for you." I gestured to the doors, standing from my chair.

"Well, hold...hold on—"

"Wait, Liam, maybe he's right."

Out of everything today—the calls from the investors, Master's blatant disrespect, the runaround he'd put everyone in the office through—Ava's small, pleading voice was the only thing that sent my temper through the roof.

"*Do not* say whatever you're about to say," I warned, but she had that look in her eye and that stubborn jaw was set even as her shoulders sank.

"We've been building to this for months. It's make or break and...and, okay, maybe he's right. I'm just an assistant. I couldn't get my head around the numbers so, maybe—"

"Say one more word and I swear to God," I barked, volume loud enough to freeze most of the people hovering around the conference room doors, watching the drama unfold.

"I'm just saying—"

"I'm just saying that if the woman who's been acting as our COO since nearly the day you were hired says there's something wrong, there's probably something fucking wrong."

I was yelling now, and she was glaring at me, but I didn't care if she got pissed off. I was pissed off, too. How did she not see how brilliant she was? How was she letting the mistakes of someone else dictate her career, her future?

"Hey, man, I get it. I...I spoke out of turn, and that wasn't cool. It's been a bad night." Masters shot to his feet, skirting around Ava's chair to stand in front of me, hands raised. Contrite.

It only spiked my anger higher, fanning the flames into something close to rage. This dumb asshole thought he was playing us. The only question was, what game?

"You want the company? Yours." He continued, a line of sweat rolling down his temple now. "I'm handing you everything you want. All of it just...let's get the papers in and we'll...sign." He finished weakly, swallowing and sweaty.

I leaned closer, fighting not to wrinkle my nose at his stench. Jail cells and bad decisions. "She has been bending over backwards for weeks to make this deal work for you, and you just insulted her."

"I'm sorry—" he started, but it was too late.

"When I find out how and why you've been wasting our time, and the time of every person at this company, you will be hearing from me. Because something's wrong, and all signs point to *you*."

What was left of the blood drained from his face, leaving him pale and waxy, lips fading into his splotchy, uneven skin. "Wait, listen. I can explain. Victor said—"

"Victor said?" I cut him off, towering over him as fear, panic, washed over his expression. "Get out."

He muttered something before finally turning on his heel and fleeing, hand over his face as he fumbled for his phone. I followed him, leaning out of the conference room doors to make sure he got on the elevator and the hell away from my office.

Wide eyes stared at me from the cubicles. "Deal's off. Something's weird about that company. Sorry for the runaround, but it's business as usual today. Back to work." A beat of silence held as the doors swung shut, but before they closed fully, whispers had already broken out among the staff.

"We're going to have to explain that," I growled, pouring a glass of water from the side table and wishing it was scotch.

"We're going to have to call the partners first."

"Yeah, and every other PE firm in the city to warn them away," I agreed with Ben, my brain already laying out the next few hours of my day. The calls we'd have to make, the damage control. Ava and I could take most of it so Ben could get back to vacation...

"What did he mean, you call me your COO?"

I lowered the water glass from my mouth without taking a drink. Ben was quiet while Ava stared, eyes unfocused on the elevator doors that had just closed on Masters' back. I swallowed, mouth dry. "I don't want to get into this right now."

Green eyes slid to mine. "You said I was your acting COO."

Ben muttered another curse as Ava sat, waiting. I could already see the anger, the betrayal, etching across her face before I'd even had a chance to say anything. I took a sip, buying time.

"Why would you say that, Liam?" Her voice bit through the air, frigid. It cut through any final hesitation I had. Enough was enough. Ben had been right all those weeks ago. This arrangement we had with her was sloppy and, maybe, dishonest. And on top of all that, I was so damned tired of her not seeing how valuable she was, not owning her worth to me and the rest of the world.

"Because you are." I slid back into my chair, knowing from the way her shoulders jerked backwards that she was preparing for a fight.

"I'm your *assistant*." She leaned forward like she could make me believe it if she just said it loud enough.

"You're not." I shrugged. There wasn't really anything else to say on the matter. She bared her teeth at me.

"I'm. Your. Assistant."

"You haven't been my assistant since your first week here. Come on, Ava." I rolled my head to work out the kinks in my neck. Everything about this horrible day crashed down all at once, a headache beginning to pound at the base of my skull. "You were prepping financial documents within your first month here. You run our finance and client outreach teams. You want *your title* to be assistant, but *you* want to run this place. So, fine, that's what we're doing here."

Her mouth dropped open. Definitely betrayal. "When were you planning on telling me this? When were you planning on *paying* me for this?"

Ben cackled as Ava's arms folded across her chest.

"You think every secretary on staff has a starting salary in the two hundreds?" My mouth twisted in an ironic grin. "You think everyone gets bonus checks on their work anniversary? When they close a deal? Hell, Ava, we gave you a bonus on your *birthday*. We're throwing money at you every chance we get to make sure you have commiserate pay because you've turned us down every single time we've tried to promote you."

"That's—" Ava sputtered, a growl working its way up her throat. "Commiserate to what?"

"To the value you bring to the organization."

"And...well," Ben started before he trailed off. A good call because I could see where he was going and didn't want to pour gasoline on that particular firestorm right now. But Ava heard it, too.

"And what? What else are you hiding?" she demanded.

Ben cleared his throat. "Commiserate to us. Or as close as we can get."

"To *you*?" She sounded like she was accusing us of something, and maybe it was deserved. I'd told myself for so long this was what she wanted, and I was just following her lead. But was I the bad guy here? I let go of the glass before it shattered under the pressure of my clenching fingers.

"You operate at an executive level. Your take-home pay is lower than ours, because of your title, but we've increased your equity as much as we could without you noticing."

Her eyes rolled. "Yes, I know because I'm more hands-on, I get slightly more equity in our portfolio companies."

"In this company, too." I tapped my finger on the table, bracing because I knew this was probably going to rock her world. "We've been increasing your stake in Wildes."

"I think I know how much equity I—"

"We've classified your equity raises as profit sharing. You wouldn't see it unless you're looking for it," Ben sounded guilty. "It won't pay out until we sell some of our portfolio companies, and the Wildes equity...won't pay out until we do something big."

"Which we will, because ever since you came on board, we've been growing faster than we ever thought possible." Did I sound guilty, too?

"How high?"

Ben quoted the number from memory, and her eyes bugged out of her head. She shoved back from the table to pace the floor. "That's too much."

"It's really not enough," I laughed, even though my lungs felt raw. The way she was moving, frowning, looking at me like she didn't recognize me. I hated all of it.

There was a reason we'd kept this from her. I could see the panic starting to flare in her eyes.

"I...that's...I can't..." Her hands flew up as she pressed her fingertips to her forehead. "I'm your *secretary*."

"You take first passes on contracts, manage our portfolio clients, direct due diligence. Wesley wouldn't be able to function without you, so let's add event management and marketing under you, too. *You* have your *own* secretary."

"Cheryl? She's *your* secretary."

"She sure as hell doesn't report to me. I hired her for you, Ava. Because you don't know how to sit still, and you always take on too much. You want us to call you a secretary, fine, but honestly, I'm tired of you not realizing what you're bringing to the table here."

"Because you've been lying to me." Her lips quivered.

"I didn't lie outright." Was I trying to convince her, or myself? I wasn't sure. "You needed a safe place to land when you came here." I ran frustrated fingers through my hair. "I don't care what your title is. I need you to appreciate yourself as much as I do. We want to make you an equal partner. Even split between the three of us, but we're terrified you'll run off and become a barista or some shit as soon as we offer you a bigger title."

"Because you think I can't handle the pressure?"

"Because *you* have convinced yourself you can't handle it!" My voice boomed in the room.

Silence was her only answer. Everyday office sounds filtered in, phones ringing, people whispering. Ava's breathing, harsh and uneven. "This is fucked up."

"Ava," I sounded hoarse, but she just shook her head, yanking the door open to flee down the hallway. I stared at her retreating form as the glass door closed.

"She's gone?" Ben asked. I swallowed, mouth dry again.

"Yeah. She's gone."

Chapter 17
Ava

I nearly regretted my decision to hide out at Dragon as soon as I opened the door and the receptionist pleasantly asked, "Ms. Anderson, hello. Will Mr. Wildes be joining you this afternoon?"

I tried not to glare. It wasn't her fault I couldn't go to my apartment. It would be the first place Liam would look. And he *would* look, it was only a matter of time.

I doubted he'd expect me to come to Dragon without him, and the club had the one thing I wanted right now. But I couldn't even take two steps into the door without hearing his name.

"No, he will not."

I didn't want to be associated with Liam, didn't want people to think I'd drop to my knees at a snap of his fingers. Not when, despite everything that had occurred between us over the last few weeks, he had lied to me. For years. Or at the very least, hidden the truth of *my own job* from me. It was enough to make me want to hulk out and smash the hostess booth to smithereens. Not very sub-y of me.

I heaved a breath into my lungs, willing my hands to unclench and my face to straighten itself out. Because unlike Liam's very misguided belief, I wasn't constantly set on a hairpin trigger. I could handle tough shit. I was a tough girl.

"Is Whitney here?"

I was a tough girl who needed her best friend, and that was fine. I'd been through enough therapy to know that my darkest times were when I'd refused to ask for help. And even though the thought flitted through my mind that I'd been doing just that for months whenever Liam asked me how work was going, I crumpled it up, tore it to shreds and shoved it down to the darkest, farthest corners of my brain.

I didn't need that type of clarity stinking up my perfectly righteous fit of rage.

"Sorry. Whitney switched her shifts this afternoon. She'll be in around ten tonight, if you'd like to come back then?"

Damn. "No, that's...fine. Let me just..." I pulled my phone out to text her. I really didn't want to go back to my apartment. I felt like a fish in a barrel there, and Liam knew to check across the hall if I wasn't at my place.

"Ava?"

My eyes shuttered closed. Just like it had a few weeks ago, my heart shoved itself up my throat at the sound of Andrea's voice. But for some reason I couldn't fathom, I was more concerned about Andrea seeing me like this—frazzled and pissed—than kneeling in a nightie.

"Andrea," I pasted a smile on my face, but her look told me she saw right through me.

"You look...peaky. All this business with Masters? Nasty stuff."

My laugh sounded forced, and I glanced back down at my phone. Nothing from Whitney. A wave of prickly heat washed down my neck. "Well, yeah, that's a shitshow. I...we're still...You know it's..."

Andrea's weighted attention was a tangible feeling on my skin. My phone screen remained blank.

"I mean, I had it handled, but if Liam weren't such a high-handed *asshole* dead set on *keeping things* from me and undermining weeks' worth of work, maybe I'd look a bit less *peaky.*"

The server's eyes went round, and I wondered faintly if this was the first time a sub had ever disparaged her Dom in the club before. Mistress Giselle ran a tight ship, low drama. And here I was, wrecking ball Ava, blasting all that lovely balance and pristine matching history into smithereens.

That and probably any chance I had of wooing Andrea over to our side. I was an emotional mess, and the thought sent those heated prickles roving down my spine to congeal in a hot pool of shame in my stomach.

Was this the same as before? One professional mishap and I fell to pieces? I should ask the nice hostess to call an ambulance now. Apparently, I'd learned nothing in the four years since my *last* emotional blowup.

I pressed a knuckle between my eyes, cursing. "I'm sorry. I just came here to see my friend. Now is not the time to…" To word vomit all over a potential investor? To get a reputation as a mouthy sub at the best club in the city? To fall apart?

My fingers smoothed across my forehead into my hair. If it looked anything like I felt, it was probably standing on end. "I apologize," I started again, taking a deep breath, then another when the first did nothing to quell the raging inferno in my brain. Liam had *lied.* I'd thought he was more than my boss. I considered him one of my closest friends, and this past weekend, I'd allowed myself to think maybe, just maybe, more.

Had it really only been this morning I'd woken up in his bed feeling like everything was right with the world? "I should—"

"You should come have a drink with me. Seems like it's been a busy day." Andrea sounded like she was smiling, but I couldn't force myself to look at her. I was more a teeming pile of fire ants than I was myself, and I didn't want her to see that. I didn't even want *me* to see that.

"Thank you, but I'm just here to see—"

"A friend." Her feet edged into my line of sight. Pristine navy suede pumps I'd have coveted in a heartbeat if I'd had any extra room in my head. "We've been talking business on and off for the last year, and I've seen you during a scene, I think we can call ourselves friends, don't you?"

I swallowed against a hard lump in my throat. There was too much emotion rioting in too many corners of my body. My phone screen was still blank, and usually if Whitney wasn't around, I'd have called Liam. But that wasn't an option today.

"Come on. We'll put it on Liam's tab."

I didn't know what sort of petty bitch it made me, but that finally did the trick. Liam had pissed me off so much, I wasn't sure my thoughts were my own anymore. Just a corrosive cloud of ash spewing from my brain at random intervals. The least he could do was buy me a drink.

***

We started with Vested, because that was the easiest. I unloaded the day's events as we settled into a low set of club chairs at the back of a small side lounge.

"I never liked Masters." Andrea took a sip of her martini when I'd finished. "I met him at an event a few months ago, and he blatantly ignored me to speak to one of my male colleagues all night. And he looked greasy."

"He *is* greasy," I agreed, picking up one of the truffle fries she'd ordered, only to drop it back in the basket. "Something is off there, and I should have seen it."

"Don't let that man undermine your confidence." I might have brushed Andrea's words off as an empty platitude, but she sounded so exasperated, I had no choice but to pay attention. "You're very skilled at what you do, but you don't have to know everything under the sun. No one does."

Her words settled like stones in my stomach, reminding me of all the other things I hadn't known until just an hour ago. Her sharp eyes narrowed over her glass.

"This isn't just about Masters, though. You mentioned Liam."

I dragged a sip of the vodka into my mouth. I didn't want to go into this, not with her. I still felt too pissed and spiky. Unstable. "I shouldn't complain about work stuff. It's fine."

"If you're worried about spilling the tea to a potential investor, you'll find I have a remarkable knack for separating what happens in this club with what happens outside the door. Tell me, or don't, but I'm here if you'd like a nonjudgemental ear."

She gazed at me steadily while she popped another fry into her mouth. For some reason, I believed her. And I needed someone to listen without judgement.

Whitney would take my side, but she'd probably only consider my argument with Liam within the context of our D/s relationship. Ben might be someone I could count on, but he'd been in on it all, too. And here, right in front of me, was someone who could understand both the business *and* personal implications of the biggest fight Liam and I'd ever had.

I took a breath, balling my fingers in my lap. "Liam said I was Wildes' acting COO."

Andrea hummed, nodding like this was the least surprising thing she'd heard all day. I waited a beat, until her eyebrow twitched. "And?"

"And...and *you knew*?" I demanded, watching as her surprise over-rode her Botox and her brows lifted a full centimeter.

"You didn't?" Her wide eyes, her obvious shock. It was abruptly too much for me to handle because, if she knew...

"Did everyone know but me?" I whispered, my voice harsh and raking. "Oh, my God, what must people be saying about me? All my clients, investors..." I covered my face with my hands because all at once, I had a name for that restless, barbed heat tearing my insides up.

Embarrassment.

Yes, I was pissed at Liam, and yes, I was hurt, but mostly all I felt was ashamed. That he'd pulled one over on me. That I hadn't *seen* it. That I'd been so absorbed with keeping myself in my little secretary box, it had never occurred to me to look up and get some freaking perspective.

And all of that crashed over me on repeat, rising and surging with everyone I pictured in my head. Wildes' staff. Holmes. *Victor*. Our investors, our prospects. I was a laughingstock. A woman so sure she had everything under control, but didn't even know her own job title.

"Would you like to know what we say about you? Your situation?" Andrea's voice was so soft, it made my eyes water. I pinched fingers into them. If I cried right now, I might never respect myself again. Even if I didn't, the prognosis wasn't good.

"No, thank you." I really didn't want to know what people said about me. The gossip and whispers that must follow me around while I trailed Liam at the dinners and meetings. What people must think.

"I'm going to tell you anyway." She sounded so kind, it was cruel. "Take a sip. Brace up." She watched as I took a gulp just to appease her. "We say you're one of the best in the business, and Liam's damn lucky to have you. We talk about how good your instincts are, the skills you've developed so early in your career."

She laid her hand across the table, close to mine, like she was lending support from a few inches away. "We discuss how we don't understand the dynamic at Wildes, or what you and Liam have worked out. But we know it works. Most people who've seen you in action don't question it anymore."

"Anymore." The word was dull, flat, as it came out of my mouth. Andrea raised a graceful shoulder.

"You have an unorthodox arrangement. It's natural for people to wonder." She sounded so dismissive, it was hard not to laugh at the ridiculousness of it.

"Sure, but they're wondering about *me*. Talking about my *career*. How can anyone take me seriously?" The sneaking, slithering, insidious voices in my head were quick to point out that probably no one did. I was Liam's little pet he trotted out and allowed to draft contracts every once in a while.

I was no better than Winston, rolling over for a liver treat.

"Oh, people take you very seriously. Never doubt that. Your work at Wildes has grown it threefold what Liam and Ben could have done on their own. And Liam won't tolerate any disrespect towards you."

I scoffed, throwing back another sip of my drink only to find it empty. "Sure, I've seen him lay into a CEO because the man was staring at my ass. But Liam has also been *lying to me* almost the whole time I've worked for him. It's not like he's a hero."

She hummed again. "I don't want to assume anything. I know very little about why you and Liam have the arrangement that you do. I don't know if he's lied to you or not, so I can't weigh in on that."

The bartender set another round of drinks in front of us. I should stop. I didn't want this bristly, uncontrollable feeling to get even more uncontrollable, but something about the fries and Andrea's calm, no-nonsense presence was actually soothing some of my runaway emotions.

I took a sip. It made it easier to start, to explain everything. How little I'd thought of myself after my career implosion at Nexus. How it had been so easy at Wildes to just work the way I wanted to, without all the pressure. The offered promotions, the fear that kicked up every time Liam mentioned them. And finally, this. This realization that I'd thought everything was perfect, but I'd been existing in some sort of fake reality.

We sat in silence for long minutes after I was done. Me, sorting through all the history and feelings and mentally berating myself for being an idiot. Her, quietly gazing at the art over the room's mantle and considering.

"They weren't completely honest with you," she began, her attention drifting from the walls back to my face. "But is it possible Liam never lied to you outright?"

She held a hand up as I opened my mouth to argue.

"Is it possible he just made a very safe space for you to lie to yourself?"

My bottom lip hung open for a moment before I snapped it shut. I stared at her. She stared back. Took a sip of her drink. Ate another French fry.

She was right, obviously. When she said it, it became stupidly clear. He hadn't explicitly lied to me, no. He'd only done all this because of my own hardheaded blindness. If I had just listened to him when he'd wanted me to step into a different role, who knows where we'd be now?

The thought churned the fries and vodka sitting in my stomach. "I'm afraid I won't be able to take the pressure again. That I'm not cut out for something at the executive level." And when I said that out loud, it seemed so simple, too. This single fear that had been holding me back, keeping me in the dark all these years, simply because I'd been too afraid to face another challenge and fail.

Andrea nodded, taking the confession with a gravity that made me feel understood. Seen. "If you're happy where you are, stay there. If you'd like to do less, do less. But I think you're the only person you work with who believes you don't have what it takes to be an exceptional chief operating officer."

What had Liam said? *You have convinced yourself you can't handle it.*

"I..." I was thinking about too many things. About Liam and myself, and my career and how I hadn't thought a person could be more embarrassed than I'd been earlier, but now I realized I had probably missed out on so much, just because I'd been too afraid to take a chance again. "What would people even say?"

If I became COO at Wildes, if I left. If I stayed Liam's secretary with business benefits. His sub. I didn't know which I was asking about, but I got the feeling Andrea understood.

Especially when she cackled, throwing her hands in the air. "Screw people! Who cares what they say? You grow your businesses, you make opportunities for employment and help entrepreneurs reach their goals. Yes, you also make a lot of money while you do it, but you've still managed to hold onto your soul, which is a feat in and of itself. Who cares what anyone else says or thinks? What do *you* want?"

"I don't want to be scared anymore." The answer popped out before I'd fully processed it, but it felt so good, so cathartic to say it out loud, I said it again. "I don't want to be afraid of failing. I don't want it to be like a repeat of Nexus."

"Does it feel like Nexus?"

Liam was everything Victor wasn't, and he'd built Wildes to be the same. A place where it was okay to be different, think differently. He supported me more than...more than I'd supported myself, even. When I'd been at my lowest, he'd picked me up, no questions asked, and did everything he could to give me the tools to dig myself out of that hole.

Actively did a lot of digging, himself, when I got in over my head sometimes.

"No. It doesn't."

She nodded like she'd already known that, too.

"I want to work with Liam." Still, even after all this. We'd have to talk, of course, but I couldn't imagine my days without him. Didn't want to be somewhere besides the company he'd built, the one he let me build right beside him. "I want...to be COO."

I nearly choked on the words as fear swamped me. It seemed like too much, like I was asking to fail again. But Andrea just kept nodding. The encouragement was enough to spur me on.

"And I want to be his sub. Here."

"You two play very well together, I'll give you that."

"And I want...I want..." I wanted my freaking VestedAI deal to pull through, but I knew there was no hope for that. Not after today. Not after it was so clear that nothing about Masters or his company had been what it seemed.

Why didn't I see that? Maybe if I'd paid more attention, followed more of the leads that pointed to something being off...

I stilled as Andrea waited for me to speak. Her head shifted as I sat forward.

"I want...I want to make some calls." Pieces were shifting in my head, a bright and terrifying possibility I didn't want to examine too closely. Not until I had more information.

Her eyes looked left and right, like I'd finally surprised her. "Alright. Anything I can help with?"

"You have been more helpful than you could imagine. I know you didn't expect to listen to me yap at you for an hour, but I can't begin to thank you." My head felt clear. All that hot, nauseous lava in my blood had settled into the familiar, focused feeling of a next step, a plan. "I know you said you wouldn't bring this out into the real world, but I truly hope my falling apart hasn't impacted your decision of whether or not you want to work with Wildes."

Because if I was going to do this, take this step, I'd take any ally in my corner I could possibly get.

"Oh, I'm sorry, this conversation certainly has affected my decision." She smiled before my heart could drop. "I like you, Ava. And I like working with people I like. Call me when you officially get that promotion."

She stood when I did, and I couldn't help myself. I reached out and pulled her into a hug. Somewhere in the business corner of my brain, something was screaming. Hugs were not professional, and I had an image to maintain.

But right now, my image didn't matter. Maybe it never really had. All that mattered was I was a woman who'd found a friend when she needed it. A sub who needed the reassurance of a Domme before something scary happened.

A person who needed another person.

Later, my phone rang as I set up my laptop on a sleek wooden table. "I'm so sorry, I just got your texts! I was getting my nails done. Where are you? What do you mean Liam's been lying to you?" Whitney sounded worried and rushed.

I let out a shaky breath because it seemed like days ago I'd sent those messages, not hours. "It's okay. There have been some developments. I'm doing some work but you can find me later and I'll catch you up."

"I'm heading to the apartment now. I can come right over."

"I'm not at the apartment." I glanced around at the plush comforter on the bed and the brocade wallpaper. "I'm going to need you to watch Winston for one more night."

Chapter 18
Liam

Ava didn't come back into the office that day, and when she didn't answer my calls or texts, I decided to give her some time.

Maybe she'd use the space to think about everything we'd done together, how successful we'd been and how close we'd gotten. Maybe she'd hate me for not being more forthcoming with the truth of her role at Wildes. Maybe she'd leave.

The thought had haunted me as persistently as her scent in my bed as I tossed and turned that night.

I'd thought I was doing the right thing, giving her what she wanted, giving her space to get her confidence back with her career. But was I just as bad as Victor? Had I selfishly kept taking everything she had to offer without giving her what she deserved?

I'd told myself I was just taking off the pressure that came with a big title, helping her focus on the work she loved.

Like a Dom would do, taking care of his sub without her having to ask. Maybe without her even knowing what she needed.

But I hadn't been her Dom then. I wasn't sure I was now, either.

Now, I was just a desperate man, standing on her doorstep with her favorite coffee in hand, praying she'd answer my knock as the morning sun crested the skyline.

"She's not there." I turned at Whitney's voice, just in time to see Winston bound out of her apartment. I reached down to rub his head.

"You've seen her?"

"And picked up the pieces a little bit, yeah." Whitney's head tilted as she peered at me. "You hurt her, Liam."

I sighed, chin dropping to my chest. "I know. Do I get any credit at all that the thing she's pissed about will make her millions of dollars?"

Her curlers trembled as she shook her head. "You know as well as I do that trust is more valuable than gold."

Shit. "Yeah. I know." I looked up and down the hallway, wishing with every fiber of my being that Ava would appear. Knowing she wouldn't. "Listen, I'll take Winston off your hands. You're a good neighbor for taking care of him this weekend and while she's...going through this."

Whitney's eyes slitted and she stepped more fully into the hall. "You planning on holding him hostage?"

"Obviously. She's not going to come near me unless I have something she wants." My mouth twisted to the side. "If she quits, I'd like her resignation in person."

Whitney pursed her lips, nose wrinkling. "You have more leverage here than you think you do, with or without Winston." That should have been comforting, but all I could think was that Ava was gone and I had no clue where she was, what she was thinking, and if I'd be able to fix what I'd ruined.

"Does that mean you won't give me the dog?"

Whitney tossed Winston's leash at me. "When she finally comes around, you'd better grovel like your life depends on it."

"Trust me, I'm planning to." Because my life, my business, my *happiness*, very well might.

***

"The latest reports on Holmes' accounts, sir." Cheryl slid the folder across my desk harder than usual. They made a fluttering, smacking sound as they hit the wood.

I glanced up from my computer screen. "You mad at me, too?"

She sniffed. "You should have told her."

I wasn't surprised Cheryl knew what had happened. Ava had managed to reschedule every single one of our meetings today, and she'd probably had help. I was looking at suspect number one.

"Yes. And she should have had the balls to take every promotion we attempted to give her. I'll still take responsibility, though." I should have been upfront with Ava from the beginning. I could see that now, and swore I'd never keep anything from her again, if she just gave me another chance.

Cheryl's eyes turned squinty. She and I usually had a good rapport. She understood without me having to spell it out that she was here to support Ava, not me, but our work was so entwined, Cheryl ended up crossing over when it was warranted. She was competent, but kind, and I wasn't used to her looking at me like I'd run over her cat.

"If she leaves, I'm going with her," she stated, looking at me like she thought I'd argue.

I slumped. "Same."

The clock on my desk ticked as Cheryl studied me the way Whitney had earlier today. "Does she know you love her?"

I blinked at the usually soft-spoken woman. "No." I sounded hoarse. Cheryl's mouth twitched.

"Maybe you get that out in the open, too, before it bites you in the ass."

I cleared my throat, partially to hide the laugh that caught me off guard. "I'll take that into consideration."

"Well," she sniffed again, straightening her skirt. "Consider quickly. She'll be here at three-thirty and said there'd be hell to pay if you weren't at your desk waiting for her."

I startled, straightening in my chair as my gaze whipped to the clock. "That's now. She's coming in right now?"

"Yes, sir. And look at that. You're at your desk and everything." She turned to walk out of my office just as the doors opened. My heart jumped in my chest, throat tight as...Ben walked in. I sagged back into my chair.

"Don't look so happy to see me." He nodded to Cheryl as she walked out, leaving the door open as she left.

"You're supposed to be on vacation."

"While the company is imploding? No thanks. We turned the ship around last night." He shrugged when I frowned at him. "The kids were starting to get antsy anyway. We only cut it one day short."

"You shouldn't have to cut your anniversary vacation short. This is my fault. I should be the one on the hook to fix it."

Ben frowned. "We both decided to keep our plans from her, the equity. It's on both of us. That's what partners are for, right?"

I sighed. It was nice to have someone to share the burden with, even though I couldn't help but feel that my personal relationship with Ava landed more of the blame at my feet. "Thanks, man. She's supposed to be here soon. Hopefully she's willing to talk."

"Yeah, she texted me when I told her I was coming back early."

"She responded to you?" I wasn't jealous. Really. *Damn*, I'd royally messed this up.

"Told me not to come in early, but if I was already on my way that I should be around for this." His lips twitched. "Do you think this is when she tells us she's starting her own firm and taking all our clients with her?"

"Not yet, but don't think it hasn't crossed my mind." She strode in, hair floating, heels snapping. She'd changed since yesterday, and she looked as sharp and buttoned-up as ever, but her green eyes were tired. Had she tossed and turned as much as I had last night?

"Ava," I started, jumping to my feet. She brushed me off with a wave of her hand, gesturing behind her to the man that followed. He glanced around like he wasn't sure he was supposed to be here.

"You'll remember Cameron Hawks, Masters' former business partner?"

"Sure." I remembered his awkward posture and the beat-up sneakers. She'd been gone for a full day and brought back a software developer? I shook hands when the man offered his, my eyes still on Ava as she settled into the settee against the wall. Where she always sat. I knew she felt my gaze, but her attention was fixed on Hawks as she folded her fingers over her crossed knees.

"Cameron, do you want to give these two a recap of what we've been discussing?"

The man cleared his throat as he sank into the chair next to Ben. "Well, I wasn't sure how Mark was distorting his numbers to have so many people interested in buying the company, but when Ava showed me—"

I rounded the desk, unable to sit still, not with her *right there* and so many unanswered questions between us.

"How about you start closer to the beginning, Cam?" She urged. Her casual use of his nickname raised my hackles. Where had she been for the last twenty-four hours, and how much of it had been spent with *Cam*? And why? I winced, hating the irrational jealousy flooding my body, but I wanted this man out of my office. Ben, too. I needed to explain, to apologize to her one-on-one. Beg a little.

"Oh, right, um...Well, I started playing around with the algorithm in college and after a while I realized I'd really hit on something, you know? Mark overheard me talking about it to some friends, and he had all the business background I didn't. I'm just a coder. I didn't know what to do with it next. So, we signed on as partners, with him owning the business side and me owning the tech side.

"Once we got started, it really took off. Mark was hiring all these people; we had offices and everything. I wasn't really paying attention. I was just the computer guy." Cameron peered up at me like what he was saying was vitally important.

"Okay." I was listening. I was only half-interested, but I *was* listening. In my mind, the VestedAI deal was dead. So why was Ava dragging this guy in here to beat a dead horse?

"Well, we started defaulting on loans. Mark kept on saying we had to spend money to make money, or something like that, but the first notice came, then the next, then the next, and I had co-signed everything. When I finally started paying attention, I realized we were just...broke."

My brow furrowed. Ava was gazing at the tips of her shoes, silent. "The product didn't work?"

Cameron looked personally affronted. "The product works. The algorithm is solid. We just didn't have the users, or the cash on-hand to cover our bills. When I realized how deep we were, I wanted out. I sold my part of the business stuff to Mark and cut all my losses."

"We already know this. Ever since then, he's been trying to sell the algorithm. I assume to pay all those debts," Ben shook his head as Cameron sat forward.

"No, sorry, I'm not good at...talking. You didn't hear me before. Mark owned the business side, and I owned the tech side."

Finally, Ava's head lifted to look at me, cat eyes sharp as Cameron's words finally sank in. I leaned against the desk, looking between the two of them in disbelief.

"You own the algorithm? Outright?"

Cameron shrugged. "Yeah. It's mine. My roommate from grad school is a lawyer, and he helped me draft everything when we started the company. Mark assumed the technology could be replicated. As if a highly sophisticated AI model I worked on for *years* could just be spun up in a few months." He scoffed. "When it became clear the app didn't work anymore, and he wouldn't be able to get it working any time soon, he started looking to sell. Aggressively."

"Bring it home, Cameron." The soft smile on Ava's mouth flipped my heart in my chest.

"Like I said, I didn't know what he was doing to make everyone go crazy over the business when the app didn't work and he hardly had any users."

"The user numbers were strong. That's what we found," I assured him, because every PE firm in the city had looked into it, and we'd all come up with the same conclusion: VestedAI was hitting it big, and we all wanted a piece of the action.

Cameron shook his head again. "That's what Ava showed me. The user-base he gave you is wrong. We had a lot of people sign up in the early days when we were doing free accounts, but they all started falling off once I pulled the tech. I still had friends that worked over there, and they said they lost almost all their active users in a month."

"And when was this?"

"About six months ago."

Ben guffawed. "When he started trying to sell."

"That's why the numbers weren't adding up. He was reporting on old user accounts, the free subscription models, but they weren't active, paying users." Ava's chin lifted. "Technically, he was correct. VestedAI *has* had that many accounts before, but they aren't making money off them. That's why the revenue didn't add up."

"I didn't know that's what he was doing, so when I started trying to warn people his app wasn't what it seemed, I didn't have any proof. People wrote me off as a jilted business partner."

Guilt squirmed in my chest. *We* had written him off, too. "So, what are you doing with it now? The algorithm?"

"Well," Cameron rubbed his hands together. "I started up my own company. Just me and a few folks in my basement, really. Our app works great but...like I said, I'm not good at the business side of things. We have a few users but it's not like what we had in the early days at Vested."

"I should have seen it. If I had listened to your warnings, none of this would have blown up the way it did." Ava was back to staring at her shoes.

"We had a whole team working on this. No one saw it. And no one else looked into Cameron's warnings, either. This isn't solely on you, Ava."

Something unreadable flashed across her face. It was gone before I could decipher what she was thinking.

"Cameron," she stood, striding across the room. "As Wildes Capital's chief operating officer, I'd like to extend an offer to buy your company."

My eyebrows shot up and Ben jerked back in his seat. Cameron's mouth fell open. "I thought you just wanted me to tell them what happened."

"That was helpful, but the only thing we've wanted since the start is the technology. We believe in what you're doing—giving people an easy way to get into the investment game, democratizing access that only one-percenters have had up until this point. We've always believed in it. I assume that if we have our business teams come in and manage the day-to-day, that will free you up to work on it more, make it even better?"

Cameron was already nodding, sagging in his chair like he couldn't believe it. That made two of us.

Ava grinned. "Then let's get a contract together so we can all make a shit-ton of money."

"Yes, yeah, that sounds...yes, I...thank you." Cameron wrung her hand, then mine, then Ben's, babbling and looking like he'd just won the lottery.

"Ben can show you down to the finance offices. We have a lot of work to do to make you an official offer, but we can get it started."

Ben raised his eyebrows, Ava raised hers right back. He laughed as he stood from his chair to lead Cameron out of the room. "Good to have you back, Anderson."

The door closed behind them, leaving Ava and I alone.

Chapter 19
Liam

We both stayed where we were, the quiet stretching into something uncomfortable.

"You were with him yesterday?" I broke it, desperate to talk to her, to find out where she'd been, what she was thinking. To apologize.

"Partially." She perched in a chair in front of my desk, our legs mere inches away from each other. "I spent the night at Dragon."

"With Hawks?" A calm, detached part of me thought about how I'd kill him. Slowly, lots of limb-tearing. The rest of me was still lost. She'd been at the club?

She looked at me like I was an idiot. "No. I spent the night alone in one of the hotel rooms they keep on the top floor for out of town guests. Made calls, pieced all this together. They have good Wi-Fi there, great room service. I put it on your tab."

"Of course." I'd pay for her to spend the next year at Dragon if it meant keeping her.

"Once I was able to chat with Hawks, it was just a matter of reviewing his current business. He's got absolute bare-bones operations. We're going to have to do a lot of work, but I think it'll be worth it."

I didn't have it in me to think about a new project right now, not when she'd given me the opening of a lifetime.

"*We?*" She'd told Cameron she was COO. Did she mean it, or was she throwing her weight around one last time before she gave her notice and walked out our doors?

She sniffed as she pulled out her tablet. "Yes. *We* are going to make some changes around here, though."

She swiveled the tablet around to show me an org chart I hardly recognized. I took it, peering closer. It was Wildes but...different.

The departments were shifted, delineated between me, Ava, and Ben. It was almost the structure Ben and I had been considering all those months ago when we'd dreamed up the new iteration of Wildes with Ava on the C-suite with us.

"What are these blue stars?" I asked, scrolling through the chart.

"We need VPs. We're growing and I can't manage the events department on my own."

I lifted my eyes to hers. "You're going to delegate to VPs?"

She shrugged, the lightest hint of pink staining her cheeks. Anyone else would have missed it, but when it came to Ava, I missed nothing. "If we want to level up, we *all* have to level up. The three of us can't run everything. We'll burn out fast."

"Yes." *Yes.* I slumped to the edge of my desk. She was with me, she got it. "We might..." I glanced down at the screen.

"What?"

"We might want to shift some things around on this."

A laugh huffed out of her nose as she leaned back in her chair, relaxing. "Obviously. This is just a first pass. We'll have to work together to get it right."

The iPad landed on my desk. Honestly, I didn't care about the org chart right now. "Ava, listen—"

"No, *you* listen." She scowled, cutting me off. I braced myself for every ounce of her fury. "I hate that you and Ben hid all this from me. Our relationship is built on trust, Liam. Inside the office and out."

"I'm sorr—"

"But what I hate even more," her glare intensified, "is that I made it so you couldn't trust me."

My heart stuttered.

"I understand why you had to do it the way you did. I kept turning down the promotions and forcing you to work around me. I was scared, and afraid to fail again, and I let that push me so far into my own head, I couldn't see what was going on around me. I've been...oblivious. And kind of a little bitch. I hate that."

"You almost worked yourself to death at Nexus, Ava. Everyone understands that you need time to heal from that. We just...I just wanted to support you."

Her throat worked, eyes glancing away at the skyline, but not fast enough. I caught their glisten in the sunlight. "You have. You've allowed me to find myself and do it on my own terms, even though those terms were holding the business back. I appreciate that more than I can express, but I'm done with that now."

My throat was tight, my eyes prickling a bit, too. "Oh, yeah?"

"Yeah. If we do this, I have to trust you. And that doesn't mean you shielding me from myself. That means calling me on my bullshit and pushing me to be a better partner for you and Ben. It's what I'll do for you, too."

She already did it every day. Pushed us, challenged us, making us better at every turn. But the fear still churned in my gut, roiling.

"I've been terrified of losing you, Ava, almost since the day you started here. I refuse to be the asshole that doesn't realize what he has.

You push yourself too hard, and if I don't protect you, what's stopping you from going too far?"

"You have to trust me, too. To fail. To go past my limits and stumble a little. You can tell me if you're worried, if I start doing too much, but if I'm going to be your partner in this, I need you to treat me like I am."

I worked my jaw. She was right, of course, but letting other people take control wasn't in my nature. And when Ava was concerned, I found myself more protective than I'd ever been.

"It'll be an adjustment for both of us, but we can do it. Don't you think?"

I groped behind me on the desk before I came up with a sticky note and a pen. I scribbled a figure and handed it over. "Yeah, I do. I know you've turned down the last few offers we've made, but I'm hoping this will entice you to say yes?"

Her eyes went wide. "Ah, yes, that's acceptable..." She took the sticky pad from my fingers and fiddled with it while we looked at each other. "Anything else I need to know before we make this official?"

Ah, Christ. My chin dipped as I fought the wave of anxiety that pounded through my veins. I could hear my heartbeat in my ears. This whole time, I'd been keeping things from her, letting her set the pace of our work together—our relationship—out of fear. But I owed her complete honesty.

I needed to earn that trust back.

My head lifted. "I'm pretty sure I've been in love with you this whole time."

We stared at each other for a long moment. Me, standing on numb feet. Her, frozen in her chair. Finally, her eyes narrowed. "Pretty sure?"

Despite the tension of the moment, a smile tipped my lips. "I don't know the exact moment I fell for you, so I can't say for certain. But

I know you're my match, Ava. My partner, my playmate. That's why I've been so afraid to push you. I didn't want to push you away. At work, at the club...I did everything on your terms and didn't allow myself to see what I needed."

She took a deep breath, sitting forward to rest her elbows on her knees. Her fingers ruffled the sticky pad in a nervous gesture I'd never seen from her before. Apparently, this conversation was challenging even for the great Ava Anderson. The thought made me feel just brave enough to tell her.

"I need you." It was so obvious, I shouldn't have even had to say it. But I wanted everything out in the open with her. A smile flickered across her face.

"What are your terms?"

My terms? I had a lot. "I want you to be my COO. I want you to have an equal stake in this company."

"Alright. What else?"

"I want you as my sub outside of the office."

"Agreed. What else?"

I hesitated, reaching the limits of what I'd told myself I could expect. Anything from here on out would be new territory, and I wasn't sure how she'd react when I told her exactly what I needed from her.

Everything.

"Trust me, Liam."

Her keen, earnest eyes clawed into me, dragging out a request I hadn't even allowed myself to fully consider until right then. "Move in with me."

Her eyes flared as she sat back. I'd surprised her. Maybe I'd gone too far.

"It doesn't have to be now...you know what, fuck it. Yes. It should be now. You're my best friend, and my house is completely empty without you in it. If you don't like my place, we can move. Get a penthouse somewhere or something, but I love you. I want to be where you are. I want you to sleep in my bed every night while Winston snores loud enough to shake the damn windows."

The dog in question whacked his tail on his bed in the corner while Ava laughed.

"I like your house. What else?"

She hadn't said yes, but that laugh, that warmth in her eyes, made me release the last bit of fear holding me back.

"I want to take you to dinner."

Her nose crinkled. "Don't get ahead of yourself, Wildes."

I laughed, reaching for her. She came into my arms willingly, letting me hold her the way I'd wanted all along. I cupped her face.

"I don't want to just be your business partner and your Dom. I want to be with you in every way. Date you, build a life with you."

"Alright." Her face softened. "Anything else?"

I tugged her closer, running my fingers through her hair. "I don't want you to get a new office."

"You want me to keep my assistant's office?" she asked, incredulous.

"The one with the massive desk and sitting area and mini-fridge? Yeah, if you could force yourself to stay, I'd appreciate it."

"Why?"

I turned her, tugging her to rest against me so we could both look out my glass doors to where her desk chair sat empty. "I like looking up and seeing you at your desk. I like that we can hear each other's phone calls. Maybe one day, when I'm less obsessed with you, we can talk about a corner office, or something."

"Hopefully, you won't stop being obsessed with me," she mused, turning back around to wrap her arms around me. "Or possessive, more like."

I grinned as I planted a kiss on her nose, then another on her mouth. Because she was mine and I could. "I don't foresee that happening anytime soon."

"That's good. Because, same." Her fingers trailed across the tattooed skin above my collar, eyes dancing.

"Yeah?"

"Yeah, except unlike some, I keep better track of when I fall in love with someone."

I swallowed. "When?"

"The first moment I laid eyes on you. None of this 'I'm pretty sure' bullshit. I walked in here and was gone. I could probably do the math on that if you wanted. How many minutes, days, weeks."

"Well." My voice sounded rough, gritty and heavy with emotion. "You *have* always been better with numbers. I love you, Ava." I brushed my mouth across hers, savoring this moment with her. No lies, no fear, no half-truths.

Her lips curled against mine as she smiled. "I love you, too."

My tongue dipped inside her mouth because I wanted to taste those words on her lips. I groaned, pulling her closer to plunder and take. To give.

She broke away with a gasp, breath already coming heavy as she looked at me through sooty lashes. "This is nice and all, but you have paperwork to sign."

"Paperwork?" I wasn't thinking about work. I was thinking about her pants and how great they'd look on the floor.

"You owe me a raise, Wildes."

I grinned like a madman, forehead tipping against hers. "And then, dinner."

"No. Then we have other things to attend to," she corrected.

"Naked things." I peppered a line of kisses across her cheekbone.

"No," she said, running her hands up my chest. "I've been thinking about Victor. Haven't you?"

"As a rule, no. Especially not while I'm seducing someone." My teeth scraped against her jaw. I didn't want to talk about Victor right now, or anything else except maybe getting out of here.

"Yesterday in the conference room, Masters said he'd been talking to Victor."

Ah, that was true, and after Ava had stormed out of the building, I'd promptly forgotten about that comment. I pulled away, tipping her chin back. "You're not going to let me seduce you," I guessed, taking in that steely gleam in her eye.

"Not until we get to the bottom of this. I'd like a little revenge, too, if we can squeeze it in."

"Well, someone did clear my calendar today, so I'm at your disposal, if you'd like any help with that."

"I'll take any help you're willing to give." Her hands circled my waist. She looked so mischievous that if we were at the Club, I'd have paddled her strictly on principle. "What's your take on corporate espionage?"

I considered for a second, running my fingers through her hair. "I like handcuffs and trench coats."

"Close enough." She smacked a kiss on my mouth before pulling away, calling over her shoulder. "Let's get to work, Wildes!"

Chapter 20
Ava

"We're supposed to be doing covert shit," Liam complained, leaning back on the bench where we'd settled ten minutes ago.

"We *are* doing covert shit. Clark had to sneak out in between meetings."

"So, Clark did covert shit. We just met him for coffee in broad daylight. There should be a half-lit parking garage. Code names. Tr—"

"If you say trench coats again, I'm going to reset the passwords on all your devices," I warned, tipping my face back to feel the sun on my skin. I felt like I'd been running at breakneck speed since Monday morning, and had spent most of my night nose-deep in the business records and algorithm documents Cam had sent me. Between that and staring off into space thinking about Liam, sleep had been elusive at best.

Now that we had answers and a plan, it felt nice to sit still for a moment. "Apologies if the spy business isn't all you thought it would be," I continued as a light breeze flew by, teasing a few strands of my hair.

"It's not entirely without its perks."

I opened my eyes just as his fingertips stroked my hair back. In the bright, late afternoon light, he looked content, satisfied. A little wary. I'd seen this look on him before, I realized now. Mostly at the club, but other times, too. I hadn't had a name for it until today.

Love. The same swelling, overwhelming, scary, perfect feeling bubbling up in me, too. The one I'd pushed down and hidden for so long. *I love you*. Probably not the best thing to say right at this moment, but it felt like only a matter of time before it came bursting out of me again. Now that I'd said it once, it was going to be hard to contain.

"I love you, too." A soft smile curved Liam's mouth as he gazed down at me.

"We can't get gushy in the middle of an ambush," I warned, secretly dancing on the inside at how he read my mind. We'd always worked so damn well together. He felt like half of me. His hand swept up my cheek again.

"I can get gushy pretty much anywhere as long as you're around."

I groaned. "You need to focus."

"You're sure he'll be out this early?"

"Yep. Five-thirty, on the dot. Closer to four-thirty on Fridays." Victor had drilled his schedule into us underlings the whole time I'd been at Nexus, adamant that he not be disturbed once he left the office. At the time, I'd been inspired. He'd worked hard to get where he was, and fought to maintain his work-life balance. It hadn't taken long after my hospitalization to realize the truth. He was a lazy bastard.

A quick check with Clark, a colleague I kept in touch with at Nexus, had confirmed that his daily routine hadn't deviated in the last four years.

"Jesus. Like clockwork," Liam muttered, nodding to the front doors of the skyscraper, where Victor was storming out, briefcase in hand, looking like someone had pissed in his Cole Haans.

Liam and I rose as one, striding across the plaza to where Victor stomped towards a car waiting in the street.

"Victor! What a nice surprise," Liam called, stopping the man in his tracks. My old boss turned, his face going red as he swiveled around, searching, as if other people would come swarming from the benches to attack him. But this was a single-pronged attack today. Our backup would come later, in the form of our lawyers.

"Wildes. Ava." Victor blustered, fumbling for a tie he no longer had around his neck. I'd never seen him anything other than smug and sleazy. "Can't stop and chat, I have a...meeting." He tried to keep walking, but Liam sidled into his path, Winston by his side. Victor balked away from both of them.

"We won't keep you for long. And you can tell Masters we said, 'fuck you' when you see him. I assume that's who you're rushing off to meet after work hours?" I batted my lashes as Victor faced me, the lines around his mouth pinching.

"You don't know anything," he hissed, taking a purposeful step towards me, but Winston was there, a low rumble shuddering through his body. Victor stumbled back once more.

"I know more than you think. For instance, I know your portfolio companies are underperforming. Your investors are dropping like flies."

"That's not true," he snarled, keeping well away from a bristling Winston.

"It is, actually, according to...who was it you called?" I tapped my finger to my chin, turning to Liam.

"Parks, first. Then Greyson. Black...Sam Black, you know him right Victor? One of your top ten investors, I think. Halpern, too. You know, just catching up, seeing if they were interested in switching up their portfolios. Funny thing. They all are."

I clicked my tongue. "Not sure if you knew, but it's hardly ever a good sign when your largest investors are looking to jump ship, Vic."

"So what If they're willing to throw a bone to a smaller firm by having a conversation?" Victor grumbled with a curled lip. "That doesn't concern me. If you'll excuse me." He tried to step around us, but Liam was faster.

"But what about your investment companies?"

"Our companies are fine." Victor backed up again, glancing around, but between me, Liam, and Winston, there was nowhere for him to go.

"Are they, though?" I asked, not even feeling remotely guilty for the visible discomfort on Victor's face. "We reviewed Nexus's recent reports and filings. There aren't that many. Someone might think you're having a hard time selling your companies."

"There was that one," Liam interjected, innocent and helpful. "From the company you managed right before you left Nexus, right Ava?"

"Yes, we did find that. Funny, I distinctly remember you telling me you expected that communications app to sell for billions. But it only sold for 500 million. Must be hard times over there."

Victor's face reddened even more as Liam and I spoke. He was inching into tomato territory.

"Is that why your employees are so eager to talk with us about new opportunities?" Liam wondered, a picture of pure glee.

"Stay away from my employees," Victor warned, voice shaking along with his stubby, wagging finger. "They're under NDA. They can't speak about our financial details. If you harass them, I'll sue you so fast your heads will spin."

I shrugged. "We're in the market for some new VPs. A surprising number of yours are looking for new gigs. And things come up in introductory interviews, you know? Things not covered under the NDA. Like how you were looking to buy VestedAI earlier this year, but backed out for an unknown reason. Or the fact you and Masters have taken regular meetings together ever since, specifically around the time he started talking with us."

"Are you really so hard up, Vic?" Liam sighed, looking at the other man in pity. "That you actively pushed a nonviable company towards a competitor?"

"I...you...you're *wrong*. There's no *proof*." He stuttered, eyelids trembling, knuckles turning white.

While Liam had been making his calls, and I'd been making mine, the full picture had unfolded as if Victor had drawn it by hand. His companies were failing, his investors were pissed, and he'd probably panicked when he'd realized VestedAI wasn't going to save the day. So, he'd sent Masters on his merry way, straight to us.

"Nothing concrete yet, no," I agreed. That didn't matter. We had what we needed to make a case, and I wouldn't be surprised if Masters started singing like a songbird during a deposition. He was too concerned with saving his own ass to worry about Victor's. "But it *looks like* you sent Masters our way after you realized VestedAI was a dud. We'd see it as the opportunity of a lifetime, but it would cripple our reputation and our returns. We'd be less of a threat, and maybe you could even swoop in and take our unhappy partners right from under our noses to give you some much-needed cash. Sound about right?"

Corporate espionage. How dramatic. How...flattering. I knew Wildes Capital was on the brink of something great, and it was just a cherry on top that Victor was apparently worried enough to try to tank us.

Wouldn't stop us from suing the shit out of him, but still. It was nice to come out on top with him for once.

He made a phlegmy, rattling sound in his throat, a vein on his temple bulging. "All of this is...you can't...you have no proof. The investors can't tell you about our portfolio performance. Neither can the employees. Any information you collect is *illegal* and I will sue!"

"Everything we've researched is public record or not covered under existing NDAs. It's easy to see the pattern, really, if you have half a brain and an introductory understanding of how private equity works. It's truly a shame you have neither." I couldn't help the unrepentant smile that stretched across my face as Victor gaped and choked in my direction.

"But speaking of suing, we will be. Our lawyers should be on the phone with yours now, as a matter of fact. What do you know about tortious interference?" Liam waved the question away before Victor could respond. "Nevermind, actually. My lawyers can explain it to you better than I can. But I am extremely interested to see what information becomes public during litigation. Our suspicions are easily proven with the right documents."

"You can't do that!" Victor shouted, turning heads across the plaza. "A lawsuit like that, the rumors...they...you...you can't do that!"

"The rumors will what?" I asked, stepping close, Winston for once in his life in lockstep with me. Victor was actively shaking now. "Ruin you? Give people an excuse to leave your ass in the dust? Seems like you just took on more than you could chew. Some people hit their peak early."

I shouldn't have gotten so much satisfaction from the mix of rage and terror on Victor's face, but as I'd recently learned, I was a petty bitch, and this sparked so much joy, I could power the city block. A phone rang, and Liam nodded to Victor's suit pocket.

"Might want to get that. Probably your legal team having a group stroke. See you in court!" Liam gave him a jaunty wave before resting his palm on my lower back, leading me to Liam's town car waiting on the street. Behind us, Victor might have been having an aneurysm or screaming at his legal team or staring after us in shock. I honestly couldn't be bothered to look back and see.

At Liam's direction, his driver pulled into traffic, heading for my apartment. I sat back, limp. "My place, not yours?" I asked. He laced his fingers through mine.

"Yours then mine, we have to change."

My head popped up from where it had drooped on the headrest. "Change? For what?"

"Anderson, I told you. I'm taking you to dinner."

***

Sometime after the waiter served the sashimi appetizer, the giddy endorphins from our coup and the tingling first-date jitters started to notch down.

Liam had dropped me off at my house only to come back later in a crisp black shirt, cuffs rolled to his elbows, and a torturously well-tailored pair of charcoal pants. We'd matched, with my black mesh turtleneck snug over a bandeau bra and silk skirt.

As we discussed the next steps with the lawyers, I caught Liam sneaking the quickest glimpses at my partially exposed skin, then coming back for a second time, like he had to keep reminding himself he could.

We had a lot of things to unlearn when it came to each other.

"To your revenge." Liam lifted his lowball glass in a toast.

"To...us," I countered, making his eyes dance.

"To us."

I took a sip, glancing around the familiar walls of my favorite swanky sushi restaurant.

"I thought you hated this place," I commented, lining my chopsticks up with the soy sauce bowl.

Liam leaned his elbows on either side of his plate. "Why?"

"Probably something to do with the last time I wanted to order from here and you said it was overpriced and their hand rolls tasted like feet."

He teetered his head from side to side. "I stand by that, but I'm not planning on ordering hand rolls tonight, and you love it here."

"That's true." My napkin rolled between my fingers in a tight spiral. "Thank you."

"You're welcome." He paused. "Ava."

I looked up from the cloth to see Liam gazing at me like I was the most beautiful, frustrating, incredible, annoying person he'd ever met. Like he knew I was spiraling over here and dammit, he probably did because it was *Liam* and his bullshit radar was finely tuned.

I let go of my napkin, leaning across the table. "What do we talk about?" He blinked. "I mean, aside from work."

His attention turned hungry. "Eventually, we're going to discuss how it's possible for you to cover yourself in fabric but still expose almost all your body. And why, exactly, that contrast makes me want to tear your dress apart with my teeth. Expect a dissertation."

My words filtered with laughter, because he was ridiculous. "Aside from work and *sex*." I mouthed the last, glancing from side to side to make sure the other patrons weren't paying too much attention to us.

Instead of laughing, or giving me shit for not being able to say the word 'sex' in public, even though I was a card-carrying member of a kink club, he merely tilted his head. "We talk about whatever we want."

"Right, I know, but all our lives together so far have centered around work. Or sex. And outside of that...I don't know. Do we have lives outside of work and sex? I watch a lot of medical dramas," I supplied.

He popped a piece of ginger in his mouth. "Me too. Did you watch The Pitt this week?"

"No, I don't want to talk about TV, either." I wasn't sure what I wanted to talk about, but it seemed imperative that it be something new, something that would bridge all the gaps between where we'd been a month ago, and this weekend, and yesterday, and today. Something *more*.

"Okay," he drawled, frowning at me while the waiter refilled his water glass. It occurred to me that on a first date with my absolute dream man, who had already told me he loved me, I was still managing to throw off the vibes.

"I mean, I love you," I started, wanting to get back to that place, to assure him of the thing I knew to be true in my soul since the first time I'd clapped eyes on him.

"I adore you," he informed me before I could keep going. A smile twitched at my lips.

"And I want this to work."

"I will not allow this to fail." His fingers reached across the table, pushing plates and cutlery out of the way to weave through mine, holding on tight.

"And we're really good together—"

"Extraordinarily good together."

"At work and in bed, but what about other stuff? I mean, that's kind of all I have going on right now. Eventually we'll have to find other things to talk about."

His thumb smoothed across the back of my hand. "When I say we talk about whatever we want, I mean I could talk about anything with you, and it would be the best part of my day."

My heart stuttered and flipped as he reached across the table for my other hand, linking us together.

"I don't care if it's work, or play, or a hobby, or the news. I want to hear how your mind works and what you're thinking about. I want to know if you're excited about something or worried. I want to have boring conversations with you about bathroom renovations and grocery lists. I want to plan vacations and figure out the next growth phase for Wildes."

"I already know my plan for the next growth phase." Tears were flooding the backs of my eyes, but I could hold them off for a little longer. Liam grinned.

"I want to hear about that. I say we can talk about anything, Ava, because I want *everything* with you. You're the most incredible person I've ever met, so strong and driven. But so brave when you allow yourself to be vulnerable, and it has been the honor of my life for you to allow me to see those parts as well. Every facet of you is as beautiful as the last, and I want all of them."

I blinked back tears now, gripping his hands tighter. "I want all of you, too. Not just work or the club. All the in between parts. You're so steady and strong. Perfectly calm when I'm spinning a mile a minute, but we work so well together. So in sync sometimes I think it's too good to be true."

It would take work, I thought, to move into this next chapter with him. To believe it when he said he wanted all of me, even the weak, ugly parts I could hardly face myself. But at the same time, I knew I could, because I knew what he was feeling. I loved him when he was in control, and equally when he lost his temper. I loved him when he was tender and harsh and all I wanted was to keep building my catalogue of his moods and emotions and strengths and weaknesses. To know him better than anyone else on the planet, no matter what phase of growth we were in.

His fingers left mine, and he circled the table, kneeling at my side to take my face in his hands. "Sorry, I have to kiss you."

"Never apologize for that," I murmured into his mouth, clutching his neck to pull him closer. His hand slid across my ribcage, the heat from his palm making me shiver.

"We're going to be really fucking good at this, Ava. Because you and I are the best at everything we do together."

Oh. *Oh.* There it was. I sank into him, into that reminder I hadn't even known I'd needed.

It was me and Liam, my other half, the man who matched me step for step and read my mind before I even knew what I was thinking. Of course this was going to work. Not just because of all this love I had overflowing in my heart, but because we were stubborn and cared about each other. We'd do what it took to thrive together at work, at the club, and everywhere else.

Later, I leaned against him while we waited for his car to pull around. A quick shower had passed over, making the lights hazy and the street smell like oil and clean rain. He wrapped his arm around me, thumb stroking back and forth across the sheer fabric of my shirt.

"That was a good date." I snuggled in closer, breathing in his scent and his warmth and everything that made Liam my favorite person in the world. He splayed his fingers across my spine.

"It was. A shame it was so much fun. We'll obviously go out less once you move in with me."

I peered up at him. "You were serious about that, huh?"

"About keeping you naked and ready at all times for my own personal enjoyment? Dead serious."

"I could be amenable to that. No dates, though? Dinners?"

He pressed a smiling kiss to my cheek. "I didn't say no dinners. I'll throw you a few chicken nuggets every once in a while. Keep your strength up."

My lashes fluttered. "Such a good Master."

His fingers stiffened on my back. "I really am. I'm wondering if you need to be reminded." His hands snaked upwards to spear through my hair, tipping my head back, pulling just enough for me to feel the softest, sweetest burn. "Maybe we need to head to the club and make this official."

"Yes, Sir."

His eyes scraped over my face. "We'll have to renegotiate. I'm taking Fridays out of our contract. I want every night, pretty girl, any time I want."

"Any time?" Thoughts of the club, his house, *our office* flitted through my head. It was a line we said we wouldn't cross—mixing business with pleasure—but I was finding that I lived to cross lines with my boss. Now, my partner.

He dipped down, coaxing my lips open, filling me with his tongue, biting hard enough to leave a mark. I pushed closer against him just as a car slid up to the curb next to us.

"We've going to have so much fun, precious."

"I can't wait, Master."

Epilogue
Six months later

"Don't say it," Ava warned, tracking my eyes as they looked yet again at the four carats sitting on her finger. I was still getting used to seeing it there, and every time I saw it, there was only one place my mind went.

"Sorry, I think I have to."

Ava sighed, glancing up from her screen. She was backlit by the setting sun, its rays glinting off the water. We hadn't bought a boat yet, but Ben and Tommy had the right idea about renting. A few months after the biggest funding round in Wildes Capital's history, I'd convinced her to take one for a spin. A whole week of just her, me, and a very discrete crew.

When I'd proposed on the bow of the ship our first night, there hadn't been a soul around, but when we'd both turned, misty-eyed, there had been two flutes of champagne situated on the closest table. Ava called it freaky elf magic. I was just happy I hadn't run into anyone in the halls as I'd hauled her back to our suite multiple times a day. The sight of her and that ring...

"Engagement rings are *not* the same as a collar." She intoned. This wasn't the first time in the past few days we'd had this discussion.

"Ava, love. I know collars. And now I know engagement rings." It had taken weeks of working with the jeweler to get this one exactly right—a perfectly clear oval diamond with a hidden halo underneath. "They are functionally the same."

"They are *not*," she began, looking down at the ring. It threw off sparkles every time she lifted her hand, and she stared at it more than I did. And I stared a lot. Because fuck me, that was a collar, and she couldn't convince me otherwise.

"That ring says this," I waved my hand from her head to her toes, encompassing all of her as she leaned back in the lounge chair. "Belongs to me."

"That's not—"

"It means we adhere to societal expectations of exclusivity," I argued, taking her hand in mine, turning it this way and that. "And people have to respect the claim I have on you."

My eyes raised from the diamond, connecting with hers. "Married people are freaky as shit."

Her head tipped back as she let out a full, throaty laugh that coaxed an answering grin from my lips.

"Use your logic, Wildes. When we get married, will that mean I've collared you?" Her eyes narrowed on my currently empty finger, eyebrow arching.

I thought for a moment. "It's never been on my radar before, but if anyone could make it seem appealing, it would be you."

She rolled her eyes, returning to her computer, but the idea stuck around in my head. Within a month of our first date, I'd convinced her to break her lease. Now, six months later, I was still drunk on the feeling of having her in every way that I wanted. I'd rationed her for years, but I had a taste for her now. All of her. I was greedy for anything else she'd give me.

"Okay, new plan for the day. We head to shore, find a jeweler and a priest. Marry me barefoot on a beach somewhere, then have your wicked way with me." I didn't want to plan a whole wedding just to officially call her mine.

She didn't even look up. "If you want a barefoot beach sort of bride, you got the wrong girl, babe," she droned, scrolling. "Besides, I can have my wicked way with you any time I want, and I have that call with Cam in fifteen."

I slumped back into my chair. "Whose idea was it to have a working vacation, anyways?"

"We're only working half-days." Her words lilted like she was trying to reason with a toddler. "Besides, the VPs get hives when they can't get ahold of us. Think about their mental health."

"Still stupid," I grumbled, knowing I wouldn't stop her from taking her meeting. Despite his protests, Cameron Hawks was a better businessman than anyone had thought. He wouldn't take a step back from his algorithm any time soon, but with regular coaching from me and Ava, he was shaping up to be pretty decent at managing the business side, too.

When word had come out of Masters and Victor's scheming, every finance bro in the city had been abuzz. Not only did Masters absolutely shit the bed at the pivotal moment, but Wildes Capital had come out looking like the winner.

We were still locked up in litigation with Victor, but the writing was on the wall there. Once we'd slapped him with a lawsuit, everything had fallen like dominoes—investors and staff leaving, company valuations dropping overnight. Word had it the board was planning on replacing old Vic imminently.

Investors were drooling for a chance to partner with us, and we'd closed our latest funding round even higher than our biggest projections. Oh, and got a new, dynamite COO all at the same time.

Everything was...perfect. And it was mostly thanks to the woman sitting in front of me. I watched her tap on her keyboard for several moments before she finally turned to look at me. "What?"

"I want to fuck you."

Her smile turned smug, like she had my balls in the palm of her hand, which was accurate. "You always want to fuck me."

I couldn't take it anymore. She was just too unbelievable, sitting there in her flowy dress, hair blowing in the warm breeze, running a third of my company. My dick twitched as I leaned forward, gripping her face. I caught a hint of her smile before my mouth covered hers to suck on her tongue.

She tasted sweet, like the oranges we'd had with breakfast. I opened wider when she arched into me, body begging for more just as her computer chimed. She gasped as I pulled back, and for a split-second I thought she might chase me. My eyes narrowed in warning. If she went down that road, there was no way she'd be taking that call.

She gripped the edge of the table. "I need to take this," she gasped, running her fingers through her hair. I should have left her to her work, but I couldn't let that comment about having her way with me slide.

My thumb brushed her lower lip. "You have my permission, pretty girl."

Her eyes widened. We mostly held tight to the original boundaries we'd set, keeping our work life and our kink life fairly separate, but occasionally, we had fun mixing business with pleasure. And fuck it, we were on vacation.

"Do a good job on this call, and you'll get a reward. Do you want that?"

"Yes, Sir." She nodded, eyes losing a bit of that icy shrewdness she got when she was in COO mode.

"Let's see it then." I let her go, leaning back in my chair as she accepted the incoming video call, spine unusually straight.

I watched her work for long minutes, listening to her discuss the next product launch, observing how her brain worked and just...marveling. This woman, this beautiful, brilliant woman, had chosen *me*. Her ring flashed in the sun, sending rays of sparkles across my eyes and amping my lust even more.

I slid the buttons of my linen shirt open. Her eyes flicked to me again, heat rising as she scanned down my body.

Cameron rambled on, talking to her about an employee situation he wasn't sure how to deal with.

"Well, it might be too early to bring HR in," she began, doing a truly remarkable job of laying out some options for him even while her thighs clenched under the table. I trailed my fingers across the silky skin there, inching her skirt up higher.

Her throat worked in a swallow I could hear from all the way across the table. I decided to put her out of her misery.

"Cam! My man. How's it going back in the city?" I interrupted his next question, which was shaping up to be something along the lines of "how do I get the board off my back?" They'd need more time for that one.

Cameron nodded when I leaned into frame. "Hey Liam. Holding it down back here. I know I texted you when you broke the news, but congratulations again. I'm so happy for you."

He really meant it, too. In the cutthroat business world I was used to, he seemed to be the real deal—a man who cared deeply about his product and his business. He'd been the acquisition of a lifetime.

"Thanks. Listen, you mind if I steal her? I know you have a few minutes left in your call, but I've got an urgent issue, and I need all hands on deck."

"Sure. We can...we can touch base again on our next call?"

Ava cleared her throat. "Of course. It's like I keep telling you, though, you know more than you think. Trust yourself, Cam. You're doing great."

The man on the screen didn't look so sure, but his insecurities weren't my problem right now. I slapped the laptop shut as soon as he logged off, Ava practically lunging across the space separating us to land a searing kiss on my lips.

I scooped her up, striding across the ship to the suite we'd been holed up in more often than not. Ava groaned as we walked, arching in my arms and twining her fingers through my hair. I decided to allow it because it felt so damn good to have her writhing and desperate against me. I'd have to give her a spanking later, of course, but that was all part of the fun.

"Urgent issue, huh?" she panted as I kicked our bedroom door closed, pressing her up against it.

"Yeah, my dick is about to bust through my zipper." I shoved my tongue down her throat, thrusting in and out in an imitation of how I was about to invade her body. "Such a good girl. So sweet, so pretty."

"Thank you, Master," she gasped as I pressed my hips into hers, rocking her harder against the door. I hoped those crewmembers were making themselves scarce out there.

I tasted her one more time before whirling around, pressing her hands up against the door and tapping the shining rock on her finger.

"Do not take your eyes off of this. Understood?"

"Yes, Sir." She rested her forehead against the cool wood as she arched back into me, dragging her ass against my dick. I gave her a smack on her hip for the impertinence, holding her in place while I worked my zipper down.

"Look at that diamond while you get railed by your boss and think about how I own you. Completely." My teeth sank into her earlobe while I yanked her skirt up. She was already shaking as my fingers dipped between her legs, finding her ready for me like I knew she'd be.

"So wet, precious. Because you're *mine.* Now. Forever."

She jerked against the door when I thrust inside, pounding with rough, single-minded intention as she cried out and pressed against me.

It wasn't an intricate scene at Dragon, or the more gentle, vanilla lovemaking we sometimes favored at home when it was dark and quiet and it felt like the two of us were the only people in the world.

This was quick and dirty and necessary. Fast enough for me to groan, loving and hating it when she screamed, coming hard without taking her eyes off her ring.

We stared at it, both of us panting and moaning, watching it shine like a beacon as my own orgasm ripped through me. I groaned into her hair, pulsing as I emptied myself into her, petting her neck, her breasts, hips, while we both came down from the high we'd only been able to find with each other.

She sagged against the door, still looking at the diamond.

"Master?"

"Yes, pretty girl?" I kissed her temple, glistening with a sheen of sweat.

"You were right."

"What about this time?" I stroked her hair, waiting as she hesitated, narrowing her eyes in thought.

Whack.

Ava jerked, pussy clenching around me when I spanked her. The feeling nearly took me to my knees. "Prompt and honest response, Ava," I gritted, pulling her against me just to see if I could force my softening member into her further. I never wanted to leave.

"I think this is kind of like a collar."

Hmm. "And?"

"I like it. Why haven't you gotten me one before?"

I grinned against her neck, pressing kisses there as I thought about my response. She had a little ribbon she wore on her neck around the club sometimes, but we had been together long enough now that people knew we were a matched set. Besides, she excelled at subbing. She felt so much like mine that collaring her felt superfluous. Though, the engagement ring had too, and I'd still sprung for that.

"Honest answer?" I asked.

"And prompt, please."

I spanked her again, and she giggled, the sound, the feeling, wrapping around my dick. I'd be ready for round two before she knew it, if she kept that up.

"Because I don't need to put something around your neck for people to know you own me."

Her head tilted back, eyes still angled down like the perfect little sub she was. I wanted her to raise her eyes. To look at me so I could smack my palm against her ass and get this started all over again.

A smile flirted at the edges of her lips. "I think you have that backwards. Sir."

My fingers flexed in her hair, leaning her back even more, forcing her to look at me, muttering before my lips met hers, "I really, really don't."

Also by

Want more smart, empowered women and the men who love them? Check out Julia Fisher's workplace romance series, Occupational Hazards.

About the author

Romance author Julia Fisher writes about smart, relatable characters, sizzling chemistry, and life-changing love stories. She lives in Atlanta with her family, too many pets, and a massive TBR she'll never be able to work through.

Follow @JuliaFisher_Writes on TikTok and Instagram to stay up to date on the latest in the series, including release dates, bonus chapters, freebies, and more!